A Gangster's Revenge 3
The Rise of a King

Lock Down Publications
Presents
A Gangster's Revenge 3
A Novel by *Aryanna*

Lock Down Publications
P.O. Box 1482
Pine Lake, Ga 30072-1482

Visit our website at **www.lockdownpublications.com**

First Edition January 2016
Printed in the United States of America

Lock Down Publications
Like our page on Facebook: Lock Down Publications
@www.facebook.com/lockdownpublications.ldp
Cover design and layout by: Dynasty's Cover Me
Book interior design by: Shawn Walker
Edited by: Shawn Walker

This book is dedicated to all my fans.
I LOVE YOU!

Acknowledgements

Here we go again. I'm back for the third time, and I love it. All glory to God, because I am beyond blessed. I have to acknowledge and thank the foundation and base that makes up my support system: my soon-to-be wife Mrs. Belinda Diane. You put up with my shit day after day, but you never leave my side. You are the definition of love and loyalty, and I can't do this without you. I love you, my sunshine bear.

I have to thank my fans even though this book is dedicated to you, because to me your support goes beyond these words on a page. You give me hope, and I am grateful.

I have to thank all the children in my life who motivate me to be more than a gangster. Just to name a few: Micaela "Kid Doodle" Lorraine, Elizabeth "Izzy Baby" Ann, Mariah "The Amazing" Grace, Jada "My Boo" Marie, Cady "Honest Opinion" Griffin, and Junior "Hell Raiser" Matthew. To the rest of my little people, I gotchu and I, and I'll see you soon.

I have to thank my amazing godmother Monica, who helps to keep me sane. You've been my light in the dark for many years, and one "thank you" will never be enough.

Of course I have to thank all my haters (my motivators). You give me a reason to smile and you keep new material on my menu. I guess you still haven't realized that I'm hungry, LOL!

I have to thank the flagship in this storm: my Lockdown family. You push me to new height, and I love it. The game is forever ours. I would like to thank my Street Dreamerz Entertainment family. I love you all and our time will come. I have to thank my sister from another mister and my brother from another mother, Lucy and Josh. You gave me and my baby a chance to connect. I appreciate you both for that, but next time don't eat all the food, LOL!

Before I finish roll call, I have to give special thanks to my baby girl, ARYANNA. I do it for you, and I pray that one day you will know this.

Now, I would like to thank a few of the realest niggas I have met along the way. Just to name a few: Nutbutta, Ray Love, Milwaukee (Da Pimp), Black (North Memphis), Ill Will, Motey, Haiti, Just Blaze, Ratchet, Choppa, Lyve, Mookie, Diego, Shmurda, Blue, Big Haven (wood scrapping guru), The Big Hand, Smoke, Big Jack, and William Booker Jr. (you told it all). I could go on all day because I know some real niggas behind the walls. Hold your head, because if it ain't life, it ain't long.

And to my affiliates that indulge in that lifestyle, I hope you know what you are doing, because gangbanging doesn't come with a retirement plan. #LDP we in here.

Aryanna

Chapter 1

Devonte

2040

"Ooh, baby. I smell them Cinnabons, and I've got to have one! Baby? Hello, Earth to Devonte," she yelled, snapping her fingers in my face impatiently.

"What, Brianna?" I replied, giving her my attention finally. The beautiful pout on her face told me she felt some type of way about me using her first name, which she always did. I definitely wasn't in the mood to argue with her pregnant ass. Everyone knew pregnant women could be unstable, emotional, and irrational creatures. "What is it, baby?" I asked, stopping our stroll through the mall and taking her hands in my own as I brought her around to face me.

"I said I want a Cinnabon, but obviously your mind is preoccupied with more important thoughts than feeding your pregnant fiancé."

"I'm sorry, sweetheart. Let's go get you and my baby girl in there something sweet to satisfy the cravings."

"Wait," she said, holding fast when I attempted to lead her toward the Cinnabon stand.

"Yes, my love?"

"What's on your mind, babe? You seem to be zoning out on me more and more these days. Have I done something wrong?"

I searched her eyes, knowing I'd find those old insecurities swimming in them and hating myself for bringing them back to the surface. She was a good woman, a great one actually, and I knew how lucky I was to have her by my side. At the same time I understood all too well time couldn't heal every wound nor erase the scars a life of mistreatment and unappreciation has brought. "No, beautiful, you haven't done anything," I replied, taking her glowing face in my hands and kissing her tenderly on the lips. "You and our baby girl are the best things that ever happened to me."

"So what is it, baby? You know you can talk to me about anything," she said, looking at me with all the love I never thought I'd be worthy of in her beautiful hazel eyes.

I drank in that love and the beauty that accompanied it, slowly releasing my breath as I let my eyes roam lovingly over her fearless expression. Here stood my best friend, my middle school sweetheart whom I'd known forever, yet her beauty still rendered me speechless. She stood 5'7" to my 6'3" with long, flowing black curls that framed her angelic cinnamon-brown face, hazel eyes, juicy lips, and a body that was shapely enough to make me speak in tongues on many nights. She was gorgeous, but it went beyond the surface. She was hands down one of the best people I knew. Here I stood looking at the love of my life, unsure of how to put into words the turmoil inside of me.

I was on the threshold of not only turning 18, but fatherhood was only a couple months away, and I wondered constantly what type of parent I'd be. These thoughts always caused me to think of my parents, and with these thoughts came the anger and bitterness that filled my mouth even now. It had been almost thirteen years since my mom's disappearance, but how could I explain that seeing her carrying my child made the pain of that loss seem like it happened yesterday? How did I say that without her feeling some type of way? And if that wasn't enough, I had to constantly relive the nightmare that surrounded my birth, as well as the thoughts of the no-good muthafucka who contributed to it!

"Don't go inside yourself, baby. Talk to me and trust me to understand whatever is bothering you. No matter what it is, you know I'll never stop loving you," she said, gently rubbing her hand over my stubbly beard in a way that made a nigga wanna purr.

To most I seemed imposing or intimidating with my dark brown complexion, even darker eyes, and the endless tattoos covering my body. But not her. I was putty in her hands, and on some real shit I loved that, because I knew no one else I could be completely vulnerable with. "My mom has been on my mind a lot lately. I mean here we are getting ready to be parents ourselves, so it's kind of hard not to wish she was here in this moment."

"I understand, baby, and I can only imagine how hard this must be for you. My relationship with my mom is far from perfect, but at the end of the day I don't know what to do without her crazy ass. I will tell you this, though: you don't ever have to worry about me not being here for our daughter or you. And I know in my heart you'll be a better man and father than what yours was," she said, leaning up on her tiptoes and kissing me softly.

That right there proved why we were best friends and soul mates, because she knew exactly what to say and how to say it. "I love you, baby, you know that?"

"Mm, I love you too, daddy. Now will you please get a bitch a Cinnabon, because I'm damn near drooling from the aroma!"

All I could do was laugh as I reclaimed her hand and led her toward the pastry treats. "We not gonna be in here all day, woman. You know I gotta get my hair cut and get me a fresh outfit for my party tomorrow."

"I know, baby! 'Bout time your young ass became legal. Shit, I thought I was gonna end up with a case!" she replied, laughing and rubbing her stomach.

"Whatever, ma, you're only a month older than me!"

"And don't forget it," she said, half distracted by the menu as her cravings got the best of her. I decided to play it smart and stay out of her way because if the way she was biting her lip was any indication, she was about to fuck some pastries up!

It still felt kind of surreal as I stood next to her, all those years after seventh grade English class, but I loved her beyond time measurements. And while teen pregnancy wasn't ideal, I knew I couldn't have made a better decision than to go half on a baby with her crazy-ass.

I felt like doing something special for her even though I was the one turning eighteen tomorrow, just to show her how much she meant to me. Standing behind her looking at her plump ass and envisioning the tightness of her constantly-wet pussy had me wanting to do something real special right that moment, too! "Mmph, baby," I rasped in her ear, stepping up behind her and poking her with the result of my attraction.

"Nigga, don't think I won't let you bend me over in the bathroom and give me that dick while I eat my cinnabon. You know a bitch is as horny as she is hungry," she replied, laughing and grinding on my dick.

"You ain't saying nothing, slim. Grab that food and let's go," I encouraged, giving the cashier a $100 bill and not thinking twice about the change.

"Damn, nigga, you serious, huh? Well don't tease me with the dick. You better blow my back out since you rushing me and shit."

"You already know I got—" I couldn't finish my train of thought because a face from the past swam into my vision on the other side of the water fountain that was the centerpiece of the food court. I'd only seen that face once in my life, but just that one time was enough to ensure I'd never forget it. It would be almost impossible anyway. Aside from the shoulder length dreads, we could've been twins.

"Baby, go to the car," I said calmly, my eyes locking with his as he moved clearly into my view.

"What? Why?"

"No questions, just go."

"Tae, what—"

"Goddammit, Brianna, go!" I whispered furiously, but the look in his eyes said I was too late. "Oh shit," I mumbled as the light danced on the chrome .44 DE he was pointing this way. Thunder roared when he double tapped the trigger, shattering the illusion of tranquil and happy shoppers. As everyone scrambled to safety, I grabbed Brianna by the waist and not-so-gently flung her toward the open Cinnabon doorway, all the while pulling my sig p228 and letting my own series of bullets fly at my baby brother.

"Tae, what the fuck is going on?" she screamed, panic etched in ever beautiful line of her face.

My response was simple. I grabbed the snub-nose .357 out of the holster on my ankle and slid it to her, praying her survival instincts would override the panic. "Get to the car!" I yelled, stepping into the fight like an old western. This lil' nigga had heart, I'd give him that, but I hated him as much as our father, so I was more motivated.

"Come on, DJ, you bitch-ass nigga!" I yelled, taunting him while letting off five quick shots in his general direction. I could hear the return fire over the screams, but the swarm of people made it impossible to see him. Zig-zagging from left to right, I made my way closer to the water fountain, pushing people out of my way, yet managing to use the human shields they made to cover my approach. Not even bothering to pause in thought, I rounded the fountain with my finger on the trigger and blood in my eyes.

But he wasn't there.

"Devonte!" I heard her scream, and I spun around with a heart heavy with dread because I knew.

"What's shaking, big bruh?" he asked from a few feet away, one gun pointed at Brianna's head while the more sinister looking .357 snub nose was aimed at her stomach.

"This is between us, DJ," I said, hoping my voice didn't crack from the terror coursing through my veins.

"Nah, my dude," he replied, cocking the hammer on the pistol aimed at my innocent and helpless baby girl. "Ain't nobody safe."

Chapter 2

Devaughn

2027

"What the? Is my? Is that my car?" I heard her say as she came flying out the door like death was on her heels. Despite time's passage, it seemed like only yesterday I'd heard her voice, only a moment ago when it had been a voice I loved to hear and could listen to for hours on end on the phone. But those days were over.

"Shame you weren't in it, huh?" I said, stepping from the shadows and jamming my gun to her head.

Her entire body seized up at the sound of my voice, complete and utter shock radiating from her profile. For five long years she'd thought I was dead, and I was sure she'd liked it that way. But in that moment I watched her shock give way to confusion, and as she slowly turned to face me, I had the pleasure of watching that confusion trade places with an emotion I'd never seen on her beautiful face: *fear*. Real live terror swam in those big brown eyes, and that brought a sinister smile to my face.

"Dee?"

"Surprise, sis. What's wrong? Cat got your tongue, or are you just seeing dead people?" I asked, chuckling and taking the gun from her head.

She opened her mouth, but no words were spoken. What could you say to a man you thought you killed, a man you claimed to love?

"In the car, now," I growled, roughly pushing her toward the idling Maybach.

"OMG, Devaughn?" I heard someone say from the spot Keyz had just occupied.

"Mom?" I couldn't keep the surprise out of my voice, but I was able to catch my mother's falling body as she fainted like an old lady in a Baptist church.

"Get Keyz in the car," I said to one of the ten-man army I'd left the house with. Scooping my mother gently up into my arms, I walked her to the car and laid her across the seat. "Day-Day, take this gun, find Ramona, and get her back to the house A.S.A.P. I'd do it myself, but the cops will be here momentarily if those sirens approaching are any indication. Try not to let her get arrested and stay with her, because I'm sure that's who Keyz was running from, which means gunfire. Try to spin it as self-defense if you're stopped. You," I said, pointing at the closest man to me.

"Yes, sir."

"Get any and all hospital videos where the shooting took place. It shouldn't be hard to figure out on what floor all hell broke loose. I don't care what you have to do, you better get those tapes."

"Yes, sir," he replied, disappearing into the hospital.

"We got this, Dad," DD said.

This wasn't the life I wanted for her, but I could see the determination in her eyes as the firelight glowed against her skin. I knew she was a strong woman, obviously made even more so by first my absence, then what she thought was my death. Still, it didn't make my heart any less heavy as I looked into her beautiful brown eyes and dark skin so like my own.

All that shit had to end. Too much death and destruction had come into their world, but now that I had the one who'd put blood in my eye, I prayed they would know the end was near.

"You be careful."

"Always, Daddy," Day-Day said before she made her way around the front of the hospital and disappearing from view.

"Let's go!" I ordered, climbing into the car and resting my mother's head gently in my lap. "You wanna explain how my mother came to be with you?"

At first she didn't respond, simply stared at me while silent waves of tears ran like an endless river down her face. Glimpses of her in the passing streetlights showed me she was still as beautiful as ever, but both time and stress had taken their toll. Still model material, even in some tight jeans and a baggy t-shirt with her long, silky hair pulled into a hurried ponytail. It had been a while since her face saw any makeup, but her warm cocoa complexion remained flawless. It really astounded me how someone so beautiful could be so ugly inside, how such effortless grace could hide a soul so dark.

I couldn't help wondering if it was my fault. Had I corrupted her so completely when I introduced her to the game of gangbanging and all its illusions of glory? Did the blood on her hands truly belong to me, even my own that she spilled? Everyone reaches a point in life where they make the conscious decision to either obey the law, bend the law, or break the law. But in the world I introduced her to, we felt like we made the law, so I had to accept my part in the god complex I created in her. Sadly, this acceptance and harsh reality wouldn't save her life. Too much had been done, and the motto was simple: "God forgives, I don't."

"I asked you a question, Keyz," I reminded her, taking a cigar from the supply in the car's console and lighting it.

"How-how, Dee?"

"It's never polite to answer a question with a question, but I'll humor you so you can get over the shock. You didn't kill me, obviously. You did put me in a coma for five years, though. I gotta admit, that was very fucked up of you."

15

"Dee, I—"

"There's no excuse you could possibly give for the foul shit you did, bitch, so save the lame shit for a lame nigga! Now answer my question."

Once again I was met with silence, but that was okay because I could speak that language. The trick to mastering silence, beyond extreme patience, was action.

Laying my mother across the plush leather seats, I moved until I was sitting right next to Keyz. I was so close I could feel her body heat and smell the fear coming off her in waves. "Do you know the difference between someone that can kill and a killer?" I asked, slowly taking a puff of the tasty Cuban. "It's ok, I'll tell you! One does whatever he or she has to do versus the other who kills because he or she likes to do it. I guess what I am saying is, I know you have and will kill someone, but I like doing it. And I'll be honest with you, I'm gonna *love* killing you."

The last part of my statement got her attention, because she turned to face me, then, "Really, Devaughn? Do you have any idea how much I've hurt with the thought that I killed you haunting my every waking and sleeping moment? Dee, I love you."

The vicious backhand I swung demanded the rest of her sentence stay stuck in her throat. As my hand connected and her whole body rocked, I felt that old, familiar feeling of rage and blood just pumping through my veins, and I could taste its nectar on my tongue, as sweet as penny candy. This wasn't the place, though, and enjoyment had to be rendered from her demise.

Removing the phone Day-Day had given me from my pocket, I gave the voice command, "Call Sasha." It only rang twice before a somewhat familiar voice answered.

"Peace, almighty."

"Peace. Where is she?"

"Hold on."

A few seconds passed, and then I heard the confused voice of a woman I loved very much. "Hel-hello?"

"You ever made love on a million in cash?" I asked her, smiling as I remembered the first time she'd said those words to me. Candy might've been Keyz's girlfriend at the time, but from the moment I stuck my dick inside of her she belonged to me.

"Is it you?" I could hear the hope and love in every word she spoke, and it warmed what was left of my heart to know she was still mine.

"Yes, baby, and I've got a better surprise for you," I told her, putting the phone closer to Keyz so she couldn't miss her screams when I put my cigar out in the bold flesh of her face. She tried to squirm away, but I used my body to pin her to the door until the entire cherry was extinguished. "Come home, baby. This plate of revenge is still hot enough for you."

I could hear the familiar sweet melody of her laugh, which was a stark contrast to the crying Keyz was doing beside me. "I'm on the way, baby, you just be there when I get there."

"I will, sweetheart, and you're safe with 6'9", ok?"

"Ok. Dee?"

"Yes?"

"I love you."

"I love you too, my Candy Cane," I replied, disconnecting the call just as the other line beeped in.

"Speak." At first all I could make out was hysterical sobbing, which made ice of the blood in my veins. "Who is this?" I demanded.

"Mr. Mitchell, it's JuJu."

Deshana was my immediate thought, and I felt a panic unlike any I'd ever known. "What's wrong? What's wrong with my daughter?"

"She— A box came to the house. The cops— But it was Trey."

"JuJu, stop! Form a complete sentence now!"

After a deep breath, her voice came back on the line laced with tears, sorrow, and so much pain. "Deshana's boyfriend dressed like a cop and delivered a box to the house."

At the mention of this, I heard my daughter wailing in the background, emitting a sound so heart-wrenching my heart ceased to beat. "What was in it?" I heard myself say softly, not wanting to know, but needing to understand.

"It was— It— La-La's head."

Her statement was followed by a loud ringing in my ears. Then the line went dead.

So many questions raced through my mind, but I couldn't process the real information. La-La's head? No, no, no. Latavia wasn't dead. She couldn't possibly be dead because she wasn't part of this life. Keyz wouldn't—

"You? You had my daughter killed?" My voice seemed so far away even to my ears.

"It was an all-out gunfight, Dee, but I didn't mean for—"

She didn't finish that excuse before I backhanded her with the pistol, feeling her nose disintegrate beneath the gun's metal. Her screams loosened the tightness in my chest a little, but only a little. "You're gonna die slow, Kiara," I promised her with a cold, calm voice.

"Devaughn, you can't," I heard the weak voice of my mother say from her prone position. Slowly she pushed herself up until she was sitting across from me, staring at a man she used to know.

"Back to the house, now!" I commanded the driver, ignoring my mother.

"No matter what she's done, she's still your son's mother, and he needs her just as you needed me. I'm gonna choose to believe that you don't know the whole story and all that. She's—"

"Stay out of this, Mom. I like you, don't fuck that up."

"Who you think you're talking to?"

My ringing phone cut her off. "Speak."

"Daddy?"

"What's wrong, Day-Day?" I asked, hearing the tears in her voice and feeling the heavy hand of panic wanting to crush me.

"Daddy, it's Ramona. She g-got shot again, and it's bad," Day-Day sobbed into the phone.

My mind went blank, and all I could do was squeeze the comforting grip of my pistol. Fuck waiting, this bitch was gonna die *now* for all she'd done.

"Daddy, are you there?" I heard Day-Day ask from what seemed like miles away.

"Huh?"

"Daddy, there's more. I got the tapes from the man you sent in because he wanted to know if we could identify the shooter."

"It was Keyz," I mumbled, numb from the kaleidoscope of emotions hitting me all at once.

"No, Daddy. Keyz didn't shoot Ramona. It was Grandma."

I looked at the phone because it was obviously defective or my hearing was just not making sense. I told her as patiently as I could.

"Your mom. Your mom shot Ramona in the throat."

Aryanna

Chapter 3

DJ
2040

"Ouch! What are you doing, baby?"

"Don't ask dumb questions, slim. And don't call me baby, either."

"Ok, but don't just ram it inside me like that, DJ. You act like your dick is small."

"Whatever," I replied, moving deeper inside her as she spread her legs for me. I wasn't in the mood to converse. I was just trying to get my dick wet to start my day proper.

"Mmph, DJ, that feels so good," she moaned, trying to kiss me.

I smoothly ducked her advance by burying my head in her neck and giving her deeper strokes. This wasn't about making love because I didn't love her. Truthfully, I didn't know if I could ever love any woman, because experiences had taught me the opposite sex couldn't be trusted. I did love fucking them, though.

"Oh shit, baby! Y-you're in m-my stomach!"

"I'm not your, *ah*, fucking baby!" I growled, pounding her tight, juicy pussy with each word to drive my point home. She may not have been a virgin, but she was definitely tight enough to make me wanna cum fast. The way her pussy walls sucked and slurped my dick was making it hard to concentrate, but still I drove deeper and faster.

"Oh! Oh god, DJ, I'm cummin'!" she screamed to the ceiling. The warning was unnecessary, though, because before she got the words out of her mouth, I felt her cum soaking my dick, allowing me to freely push all the way inside her.

As soon as she finished cumming, I roughly flipped her over, wanting that face-down, ass-up action.

"DJ, wait," she said, trying to gain her balance by putting her hands out in front of her.

"No hands, slim," I told her, once again ramming my dick inside her and taking her breath away. Grabbing her by her thick hips, I pulled her to me while giving her all of me with savage strokes.

"Shit! Fuck me, nigga!" she screamed into the pillow.

I rode her hard and fast, the sound of our skin slapping echoing violently off the bedroom walls. "I'm about to cum," I said, grabbing a fistful of her auburn hair until her back was arched.

"Inside me! Pl-pl-please, babe!" she begged, throwing her round ass at me.

I felt the tremble start at my toes, and with blinding intensity I exploded deep inside her throbbing pussy. Pulling my dick out of her, I wiped it across her ass, then sat on the side of the bed to catch my breath.

"Damn, DJ, you know how to wake a bitch up. Next time don't stay gone for years and you won't miss the pussy so much."

"Miss you? So you think I missed you?" I asked, grabbing a blunt and lighting it.

"The way you just worked me says *hell yeah*! And you did the same thing last night, too!" she replied, laughing and laying back down.

Maybe I had missed her a little. Coco and I had known each other as kids, and even back then I knew she'd be a fine-ass red bone. She had long, curly auburn hair, hazel-green eyes, a beautiful smile, and the thickness that drove most dudes crazy. Plus she wasn't a dummy, and the sex was blazin'! The only problems were she was clingy and she couldn't have kids.

We never talked about it. I mean, she was only twenty years old and healthy, so there shouldn't have been any problems, except for the fact she'd had two abortions early in life. I'd known plenty of girls in that situation – though not saying I agreed with it – but it hadn't stopped them from getting pregnant again. I wasn't a doctor though, and I damn sure wasn't a Doctor Phil.

"Maybe I did miss you," I conceded, hitting my blunt mightily.

"So why spend so much time away?" she asked with that sexy pout most females master by sixteen.

"Come on, slim, you know why. My pops ain't playin' 'bout that education, so it is what it is."

"Now that you're graduated, what's next?"

That was a good question. Pops had college in mind, but I wanted the education of a street scholar first. And I had some things to prove, too. My pops was a legend, and I was his junior, so in my opinion those streets had to respect me. "I don't know, I just wanna catch my breath for a while."

"The sex was good," she purred, rubbing my back sensually.

"You know what I mean, Coco. I've been up top rubbing elbows with future senators and shit for so long that I just need to breath the hood again."

"Oh sure, this is real hood. You live in a mini mansion right next to your family's huge mansion, and your car cost a million, easy!" she replied, laughing.

"Let's be clear, slim, everything I got came from the blood, sweat, and tears of my family. Ain't shit sweet, and I never forget my roots. I'm not about going backward, I'm just about working for mine, too, and leaving my own kids a legacy."

My comments were met with silence, and that's when I realized where I'd gone wrong. Wanting kids meant I'd be sharing them with someone other than her. Even in the darkness of the pre-dawn light I could feel her withdrawing into herself, and I felt bad. I might not have been able to express love, but I still didn't want to hurt her unnecessarily.

Passing the blunt to her, I lay down beside her and pulled her close to me while she smoked. "Dome open," I ordered into the darkness, and a moment later the reddish-orange of the morning sky was revealed to us. I couldn't deny the beauty in watching a sun rise like that, or the way the light of a new day seemed to chase away yesterday's shadows and demons. It made me wish I could outrun all the evil that lurked in the night, but that was wishful thinking.

"DJ?"

"Yeah, babe?"

"Will you ever love me? I mean the way that I love you?"

Sometimes her questions surprised me because she was so tough on the outside, but at moments like this I was hit with the reality she was still a girl in search of love and marriage. "I don't know, Coco. All I can tell you is that I gotchu, and I always will."

Thankfully she knew when to leave well enough alone. Passing the blunt back, she slid down the bed until she was eye-level with my dick. Looking up at me, she slowly took me into her mouth and sucked gently until I was hard enough to break something. I patiently smoked, allowing her to do whatever she felt because her sucking dick was a rare occurrence for me. The sight of her visibly relaxing her throat muscles in order to take all of me in her mouth turned me on so much that I had to look away or cum.

"Damn, girl!" I murmured, putting my blunt in the ashtray and grabbing two handfuls of her hair.

"No hands, and you better look at me," she ordered, taking me back into her mouth.

The sun has started its dance across the sky, warming the room and bathing it in orange and yellow light, but all I could see was her. Again and again my dick disappeared in between her succulent lips, bringing me closer to Heaven's gates.

"Baby, I'ma cum," I warned, knowing that swallowing was not in her routine.

She stopped long enough to look me squarely in the eyes, and I saw mischief on her mind. "Good," she replied before latching back around my dick and sucking harder. That was all it took, and my world shattered as I came in great waves and uncontrollable shakes.

"W-wow!" I panted, realizing that she'd swallowed every single drop I had to offer.

"Never doubt my love for you," she said, kissing the head of my dick before getting up and going to the shower.

I had no idea what to say to that. The damn girl had left me speechless, and she was the first to do that in my eighteen years of life. Thankfully, my ringing phone diverted my attention.

"Yo?" I answered, putting my Bluetooth in and getting up to relight my blunt.

"'Sup, bruh? Sorry to hit you so early, but I figured you wanted rush delivery on that request you made."

My mind immediately switched gears when the Mad Hacker started speaking. His real name was Evy Richards, and we'd met at school a few years back, but everyone called him the Mad Hacker. The boy had skills when it came to hacking into anything, but since that crime carried an automatic life sentence, he was obsessively careful and paranoid. And he was expensive as fuck, especially if you weren't friends. He was the centerpiece of the team I'd built because without him, death and prison were guaranteed.

"It's cool, I'm up already. Whatcha know?"

"Well, he left New York last night for a short trip to Delaware with his girlfriend. And he's travelling light."

"How light?" I asked, walking to my closet to grab something to throw on.

"So light I don't even think anyone knows he's not in New York right now."

I didn't know if this was good fortune or a setup, but I'd soon find out because I was definitely answering the door when opportunity knocked. I'd spent many late nights and early mornings envisioning, plotting, and planning a family reunion for me and my dear brother, and now the time had come. "Where is he?" I asked, pulling on some sweats and a white beater.

"His hotel asleep as far as I can tell, but I don't know for how long. They're gonna notice he's gone soon."

The *they* in question were his mother's goons. The same goons had kept him safe and protected for as long as I could remember, but their days were numbered, too. What everyone seemed to forget was anyone could be touched, and when all parties involved had unlimited resources, the possibilities were endless.

"Disable the GPS in my Bugatti. I don't want my pops knowing my moves for a few hours," I said, finishing the blunt and pulling on my Timbs.

"Man, you know I fuck with you, but that's your pops. He'll kill me!"

"And what do you think he'd do just for providing this info? Get your panties out of your ass, it's time to go to work. Send the info to my car," I told him, hanging up as Coco walked back into the room, water glistening all over her beautiful body.

"Going somewhere?" she asked, lying on the bed and spreading her legs until all I saw was her pretty pink pussy.

"I'm on one, slim. Later for that," I told her, grabbing my .44DE off my nightstand.

"You need help?" she asked, sex forgotten as the ride-or-die chick in her emerged.

"Nah, get some sleep and I'll be back later," I told her, heading out the door.

"Be careful!" I heard her yell as I bounded down the stairs and into the garage.

Aryanna

Chapter 4

2040

The all-black Bugatti gleamed in the early morning light, its beauty masking the fact it was completely bulletproof. I'd learned long ago to accept my pops' paranoia because winning an argument wasn't an option.

"Garage door open," I commanded, climbing behind the wheel. "Car start. Follow quickest route to programmed location, and monitor for police." I could've easily driven myself, but I wanted the time to think about how this would all play out. I wasn't underestimating Devonte. I mean, we shared the same blood and are both students of a ruthless game. He was a street nigga through and through, and NY streets offered on hell of an education. So I was sure the nigga wasn't no bitch. A worthy opponent, I actually liked that. My hatred for him ran deep, and his day of atonement was long overdue as far as I was concerned.

I kept the speed limit until I was leaving VA, but then I opened my ride up and chased my destiny. I made it to Delaware in four hours, hoping I was still early enough to catch him sleeping.

"Talk to me," I said to the Mad Hacker when he answered my call.

"He's in the mall with his girl. You should be able to ambush him when he comes out, but what's your plan for her? She's at least eight months pregnant."

For some reason this information pissed me off more. That nigga didn't deserve to be a father. The muthafucka didn't deserve to be born his damn self! "Fuck waiting! I'm going in hot. I want you to shut down all the cameras in the mall," I said, pulling into the parking lot.

"But DJ—"

"But ass, my nigga, just do it," I barked, stepping from the car and tucking my pistol into my sweats. I knew I was moving completely irrationally, but he had to die. Period. In my haste I didn't even think to ask for his exact location, but logic said a pregnant chick was headed for the food court. I quickly made my way through the mall, my eyes scanning every face in search of the one that had haunted my dreams on many nights.

And then there he was. Our eyes locked, and for a spit second I saw my pops, but I shook that shit off as I leveled my gun at him and fired. From the first shots it was complete pandemonium, giving a visual to the phrase "running for your life." I saw him push his girl out of the way, and in that moment I saw a beautifully ugly plan come together in my mind. I could hear him yelling at me and shooting, but my objective now was to be exactly where he didn't want me to be.

I let my gun holler. Using the flow of human traffic, I scrambled around behind the Cinnabon store until I was right on top of his baby mama. "Call your man," I whispered sweetly in her ear with my pistol to her head, taking the gun she was clutching.

At the sound of his name, he turned around, his icy calm slipping momentarily and letting the scared little boy emerge.

"What's shakin', big bruh?" I asked, turning the other pistol on his unborn child, studying his reaction. I could sense the fear in his words when he said this was just between us, but he didn't understand this went way deeper than that. "Nah, my dude!" I said, cocking the .357. "Ain't nobody safe."

"Pl-please don't hurt my baby. I'm begging you," she sobbed, almost hysterical.

"Quiet down, slim, we're having a family moment," I said pushing her so she'd start walking toward him. "Put your gun down, Devonte, and I advise you not to make me repeat myself."

I could see the indecision all over his face, and his quick glances around told me he was praying for a savior of some sort. Still, he dropped his gun and reluctantly stepped away from it.

"Alright, now let her go."

"Let her go? Come on, my nigga, you been around long enough to know how this works. Besides, you should feel blessed I haven't shot you yet," I told him, moving steadily past him. The truth was I wanted to empty my clip into his fucking face, but he could only die once. This pain he and his mother caused would last a lifetime, and before his life ended I'd make him understand exactly what that felt like.

"I swear to God, if you hurt either of them—"

"Save your breath and your threats. You want your bitch back? Come get her." Taking aim, I shot him point blank in the knee, smiling at the melody his screams made.

"Tae!" she yelled, trying to go toward him, but stopped when all she could see was down the barrel of my gun.

"You can die here, if you like," I said sweetly.

Her survival instinct was blatantly clear in her eyes, swimming amongst the tears, and she kept walking toward the exit. I was sure the police would arrive any minute, which meant we had to be in the wind A.S.A.P! My pops would kill me if I got arrested. It was bad enough I'd come this far without his consent, but the happiness I felt in that moment was worth his wrath. I couldn't put into words the weight that was lifted simply by causing him a little pain, but I knew feeling like this could be addictive.

"Get in," I ordered, pushing her toward the car. "Car start. Call Evy. Did you shut the system down?"

"Yeah, but you know I watched the whole thing live. You're insane! You better get the fuck out of there because the cops are two minutes out," he said, sounding panicked.

Putting the guns in the driver's side door pocket, I dropped my car into first and smoked the tires as I shot out of the parking lot. "I'm on the move, so do what you can to clear the way, because I'm coming in extremely hot."

"Why did you kidnap his girl? Come on, DJ, that wasn't in the plans and you know it."

"Plans changed! Besides, I know what I'm doing, so let me worry about this situation."

"Yeah, well, you've got another situation. Your pops is looking for you."

All I could think was *oh shit* because that wasn't a good sign. I was raised never to believe in coincidences, which meant I was gonna have to face his wrath. "How'd you find that out?" I asked, demanding a $1.5 million performance out of my car as I hit the highway and floored it.

"Apparently he's watching you closely, because as soon as you left the radar, he started looking."

"Ok, I can handle—"

"Oh shit, oh shit, oh shit!" she screamed next to me.

"Stop all that damn hollering before I gag you!" I warned.

"My-my water broke!" she screamed.

Chapter 5

Kevin

2027

"Officers, exactly which police station are we going to? I know my father's house is in Fairfax County's jurisdiction, but we're going away from Fairfax all together."

I could hear the uncertainty in her voice, and it was obvious her nerves were already shredded by the night's activities. The darkness hid my smile, but I knew I'd have to do something or risk having to fight with her all the way to Norfolk. Truthfully, I wouldn't have minded beating this bitch to death with my bare hands, but my mother described the first piece in this chess match.

"We're going to one of the substations, Ms. Mitchell," I told her while signaling for my partner to pull over into a deserted shopping center parking lot. He was actually a real cop, and he was probably a good one, but he had kids and a wife to support, which required more than his $42,000 a year salary. Even the good guys couldn't deny the fact crime pays.

As soon as the car came to a complete stop, I was out the door with a Taser set to 50,000 volts hidden in my hand, pulling open the rear passenger door quickly. She never knew what hit her when I leveled the Taser at her pretty little head and squeezed the trigger, but her instant screams told me she felt every volt. The night air filled with her screams and my laughter as I watched her squirm and flop all around the back of the car.

"What the fuck are you doing?" he yelled, obviously panicked and worried about someone witnessing what was happening.

Police brutality was all too common for him to have anything to worry about, and I ignored him anyway because he worked for me and not the other way around. It felt good to finally inflict some pain on my enemies with my own hands instead of simply pulling strings or ordering things done. My thirst for vengeance was entirely personal, and while she may not have been the one to kill my father, it was a proven fact the sins of the parents were visited on the child.

"Kevin, chill!"

The sound of my name raised the trance I was in and allowed me to take my finger off the trigger. It wasn't my place to kill her, and the fact her eyes had rolled back into her head, coupled with the foam escaping her mouth, worried me she might be close. "You don't get off that easy, bitch," I told her.

Tossing the Taser on the floor and removing a syringe from my pocket, I quickly gave her the shot my private doctor assured me would make her as gentle as a kitten, and then I hopped back into the front seat. "Drive," I said, pulling out my phone and dialing a number.

"How'd it go?"

"There were definitely fireworks. I've got the lawyer and I'm on my way to you now."

"I'm not in Norfolk, son. I decided to follow your lead and get a front row seat."

"Mom."

"Don't *Mom* me, Kevin. This is my way, too, and I'm perfectly safe. Besides, I couldn't wait to finally do something."

I could understand her eagerness all too well, just like I understood her loss. We'd lived in our own personal hell for five years, and now it was time to invite some company over.

Nothing we could do would bring my father back, but it would damn sure make us feel better to know justice was finally ours.

"Where are you, Mom?" I asked, signaling for him to stop the car again.

"I'm at our first apartment in Manassas. Do you know how to get here?"

I was too young to remember ever having lived there, but I had often been told stories of that happy and simpler life we all shared. It was somehow poetic justice that the beginning of the end start at the beginning. "I'll be there in thirty minutes. I love you."

"Ok, I love you too, Kevin. Hurry."

Disconnecting the call, I gave him the address to Devonshire Apartments and we were on our way. I could feel the unease radiating off him, and it fed something inside me I'd been needing for quite some time. For years I'd had to pretend to be normal, I'd had to fake so many common emotions like love and empathy when all I really wanted was to peel the flesh from Deshana's bones. I couldn't express all the hatred I felt for her and her family, but I had taken satisfaction from the knowledge she'd been literally sleeping with the enemy. Maybe I'd find out if her sister's pussy was just as good or better than hers! Their father had fucked up my family, so it seemed fitting I fuck his. I let the images of Latavia in degrading sexual positions entertain me for the rest of the ride, but all too soon we'd arrived at our destination.

"Pull into that corner spot by the dumpster and kill the lights."

As soon as he hit the lights, the night enveloped us in its embrace. Everything around me seemed familiar on some level, almost comforting, and I interpreted that as a sign this was where we were supposed to be. There was a scattering of lights on in various buildings and apartments, but building 325 was completely pitch black and looming ominously in front of us.

"Grab her and let's go," I said, opening my door.

"That, uh, that wasn't part of the agreement, Kevin. All I was supposed to do was show up at the house with you in case I had to show my real credentials. This isn't my fight," he replied, staring intensely out into the night and avoiding the heat of my stare.

Closing the door without a word, I slipped the silencer I'd brought just for this occasion from my pocket. The darkness concealed my movements as I swiftly screwed the silencer onto my berretta 9mm and flipped the safety off. Opening the back door, I slid her still unconscious body to the edge of the seat, giving the impression I intended to simply scoop her up myself.

He never got to utter a sound, just slumped into the driver's side door when my gun whispered fiercely into his ear. Deep down he should've known he couldn't live after this anyway, but I'd heard cops' families were taken care of, so at least his money problems were solved.

Holstering my gun, I lifted Latavia into my arms and walked into the darkened building. The smell of her was intriguing, yet intoxicating, because it was entirely feminine with a loud overtone of gun smoke.

I was already wrestling for more time to enjoy killing her, but there was a schedule to keep to ensure the war didn't lose its momentum. I carefully made my way down the stairs to the ground level apartment where I kicked the door twice and it was quickly opened.

To my surprise there were lights on inside the apartment, and as I stepped inside, leaving the night behind, I took in my surroundings. The place was incredibly small, and the plastic lining the floor gave it a cold feeling. The windows were blacked out from the inside, which explained why no light could be seen outside.

Still holding her, I walked into what was obviously the living room/dining room area, willing a memory of some sort to manifest, but none came. There was only one bedroom, not even worthy to be called a master suite with its shaggy carpet and discolored walls.

"I know it doesn't look like much, but I have so many great memories here, son."

"Well, hopefully killing this bitch will be another for you. Have you decided how you wanna do it?" I asked, dumping her on the floor like the garbage she was.

"I just want it done and the message delivered that we're here. The days of hiding are over! Skino will be avenged, and it begins with her death," she said, kicking Latavia for emphasis.

This display of anger was rare for my mother. She was always so poised and put together, but it was understandable since she alone had held our family together after my father was murdered.

"Give me a moment to wake her up, and then we'll get started. I only have a few questions for her before you kill her."

"Ok," she replied, walking out of the bedroom and closing the door.

Some people believed death and the act of killing someone should be savored, and I was inclined to agree. However, when time didn't allow for this luxury, I believed in savoring the feeling I got from that person's fear of their immediate death. I quickly stripped her of her clothing, admiring her luscious curves and the tone build of her body. Rolling her on her side, I put flex cuffs on her before positioning her on her back. She really was beautiful. Her body was firm, yet soft in all the right places. Her titties looked ripe for the sucking, and the delicate patch of hair covering her pussy had my dick pressing tight against my zipper. There wasn't time for what I wanted to do, but a taste couldn't hurt my schedule.

With my mind made up, I kneeled in between her thick thighs, pulling my hard dick out and rubbing against her pussy lips gently. She didn't stir in the slightest, which pissed me off because I wanted her to know the honor she was receiving by sampling this dick. Maybe she just didn't deserve it then!

Standing back up, I had a sudden idea of what might help to wake her up from her slumber. Laughing softly with my dick still in hand, I began to piss on her body, guiding the powerful stream upward until it was hitting her directly in her face.

I'd almost emptied my entire bladder before she began to cough and come around. "Wh-what the fuck? What are you doing to me?" she yelled with false bravado. I could see the fear in her eyes as clearly as the tears mixed with my piss sliding down her face. I laughed harder. "Please! I didn't do shit, and I'm not a part of this war! My aunt Keyz will tell you, just call her before you do something you'll regret. Please!"

"I didn't work for Keyz. See, the problem with you people is that so many people, both innocent and those in the gang life, are affected by others' decisions. Maybe your family will realize this with your death, just maybe they'll understand my pain."

Her tears were flowing faster now, and I noticed her eyes kept going from my face to the dick in my hand. For most woman rape was the one thing they feared the most, even more so than death. It was degrading and traumatizing in a way they never forgot or escaped. It made them feel unclean in ways that stayed with them forever.

"You know, I was thinking about giving you some of this good thing, and trust me it is good. I would say ask Deshana since I've been fucking her for years, but you'll never see her again. Not in this life, anyway.

"Wait, I—"

"Don't speak when I'm speaking!" I yelled, stomping on her pussy with my boot. Her screams were as harmonic as a choir at Sunday service, and they made my dick harder still.

Kneeling again, I pushed her legs up until they were touching her chest, exposing her pussy to me in all its splendor. She tried to fight, tried to squirm and resist, but her strength didn't compare to mine.

"Please, don't!" she screamed when she felt my dick push at the door of her essence.

"Are you sure you don't want me to? It'll be your last nut ever."

"N-n-no! Don't, please don't!" she begged, shaking harder with each sob as snot entered the mix of piss and tears.

"Okay!" I replied, backing up and tucking my dick inside my pants. Still kneeling, I reached behind my back and pulled out Plan B. Her eyes showed recognition and confusion at what I was holding, and an obvious fear of the unknown. "I have a few questions for you, and I shouldn't have to tell you what being uncooperative will get you. So, where's my father's body?"

"I don't. I don't know who your father is or where he is. I told you, I'm not a part of this world!"

"Everyone in your fucking family is a part of this! None of that changes because your bitch-ass father is dead! And you goddamn well know who my father is because he was your father's direct superior, now tell me where he is!" By now I was on top of her with my hand around her throat, choking her, letting the hatred leap from my body into hers. She probably would've died right then had it not been for my mom coming into the room.

"Don't kill her yet, baby. You know as well as I do that Deshana was the one heavily into Devaughn's business. This bitch is just their mouthpiece."

I loosened my grip a little, allowing her to gulp down some much needed oxygen. The thousand-yard stare of blind panic in her eyes was making my blood pump faster, and I could feel my mouth watering as my hunger was fed a little more.

"My father is Timmy, aka, Skino the Don. He ran NTG for the east coast until he disappeared five years ago, and we know his disappearance wasn't a random accident, and you should know that everyone who helped with that abduction is now dead. All roads lead to your family. Now talk, bitch!"

"I-I don't know anything, I swear!" she pleaded.

"Then you're of no use to me." Climbing off her, I passed my mom my pistol, giving my full attention to the road flare in my hand. I pulled the end off and struck the flare to life, sending fire and smoke to the ceiling.

"Wait, you don't want me! Kill him, kill—" Her words we replaced with her pain-filled screams that echoed nicely off the walls when I shoved the blazing flare inside her pussy, and I could smell her flesh cooking. It smelled like victory. It was no secret her father was a sexual sadist when it came to murder, so this was oddly poetic.

"Shoot her, Mom!"

"Don't, pl-pl-please!" she pleaded, barely conscious from the pain.

"Thank your father when you see him," my mother said, firing a bullet into her stomach. Her death would be painful, although it wouldn't last long enough.

"Drag her into the living room while I go get the hatchet from the car," I said, leaving the room and making my way back outside. What I was feeling was indescribable, but I'd heard others use words like euphoric when they needed a word beyond happy. And the best part about all of this was our plans allowed us to pick off each person until the Mitchell family was nothing more than a vague memory.

My euphoria was short lived, though, because the look of panic on my mother's face froze me when I opened the door.

"What is it, Mom? What's wrong?"

"She's-she's dead."

"Ok, that was the plan, right?"

"In the room she said *kill him,* and I didn't understand, it didn't make sense."

"Mom, you're not making sense," I said, finally moving to her side and placing my hand on her shoulder while she knelt next to the still bleeding woman.

"He's alive. Devaughn Mitchell is still alive."

Aryanna

Chapter 6

Devonte

2040

Getting shot hurt a lot more than muthafuckas had ever told me. It wasn't a pain I could mentally prepare for unless I'd been through the shit, and I damn sure didn't plan to go through this twice! As bad as my body hurt, my heart hurt more knowing my wifey and baby girl were in danger.

I knew my father had no love for me. That was evident by everything he hadn't done for me in my life, but I didn't think the nigga would allow his son to take an innocent, pregnant woman hostage. That shit was beyond foul! I'd grown up believing there were rules to this game, but that was obviously not the case, not even amongst family.

"I can see the fire and determination in your eyes," she said, closing the hospital door behind her and moving to the seat by my bed.

I didn't respond. Instead I adverted my gaze until I was looking out into the bright sunlight. I knew I'd been wrong to travel outside of NY alone, but who could've predicted shit would go all the way left like this? Now I had to endure a lecture when I needed to be focused on getting my family back from my deranged brother.

"You know, it seems like just yesterday I was at your mother's bedside praying she'd let the hate in her heart go, hoping she'd live for you, if for no other reason. There was so much pain in her eyes, so much torment in her soul, but still she had that same determination that I see in you right now. That scares me, Tae."

I didn't know what to say to that or how to respond. We didn't talk about my mom, and I kept my memories of her closely guarded because they were mine. I never knew the full story of her life or the war that had ultimately ended up killing her, but I knew it had been going on a long time. The murder of my aunt in front of me ensured that I'd never forget, or forgive, and now I had even more reason to hate my "family."

"What do you want me to say, Grandma? I didn't ask for this shit, and I didn't start it, but now I'ma finally end it."

"Devonte, you can't go off half-cocked. Your father, he's not a nice man, and he's not to be fucked with or taken lightly. I understand how you feel."

"No, you have no idea how I fucking feel! My older life has been dictated by events beyond my control, shit that goes all the way back to before I was even born. Do you understand how powerless that has made me? My mother was a gangsta, yet here I am having to have a babysitter for my every move! Really? And as if the streets of New York ain't rough enough with plenty of enemies, I'm thrust into a war with my own blood? Nah, Grandma, you don't know how I feel. No one does. But they will. I'm grown now, so it ain't no more hand holding or kissing my boo-boo. I'm a father, and I'm a better one than your son, so that means I'ma protect mine at all costs."

"But Devonte—"

"I got here as soon as I could, homie," Ruby said, breezing through the door.

Ruby Red was my right-hand woman, the one person besides Brianna I knew I could trust above all else. We went back over ten years to the elementary school playground, and her grandfather was none other than OG Mack himself. She was NY straight up and down, Brooklyn to the core, and there was no one I needed at my back more right now. I could see the fire burning brightly in her brown eyes and could feel the anger radiating from her 5'2" frame. She was a little woman, but she packed a punch stronger than dynamite, and her fuse was lit.

"What the fuck, Tae? Who did this, and why was you alone?" she asked, climbing up on the bed next to me.

Taking her hand gave me strength, and it gave me determination, the steel backbone I needed. "We'll talk. Right now I need to get back to New York, and then straight to Virginia because the nigga has Brianna."

"Virginia? Who the fuck is stupid enough to come at…"

I could see the thought finish in her mind, and the wariness that understanding brought.

"You know who."

"But, I thought, I mean you're his son, for god's sake!"

Very few people knew the whole story about my mom and pops, but ruby knew as much as I did. I never knew how the big homies had found out, but apparently an agreement was reached that allowed my father to retire without there being an all-out blood bath. All I did know was that me and my grandma Gladys moved to NY, and that's where we'd stayed.

I was embraced by the movement, and some said I banged as hard as my mother and father combined. I still hadn't figured out if that was my gift or my curse, but before this war was over I'd definitely find out.

"As far as I know it's not my father, just my brother. I don't give a fuck who it is, they've got my family, and I'm gonna get them back. Period."

"I'm with you, my nigga. You already know Brianna is my family, too. Just like lil' mama she's carrying. We got ten of the best shooters outside, so let's—"

"Ten shooters is just ten more dead bodies going up against my son," she said from her chair. "I love you both, so

I'ma tell you what's real and what ain't. Devaughn is a monster the likes of which you haven't seen. He has the ability to disassociate himself from all emotion once he perceives you as his enemy, and he enjoys killing. Growing up as he did, killers were glorified, and that alone fucked up his moral compass. Make no mistake, sweetheart, he will kill you without hesitation."

I could see both the worry and resignation on her face. "So what am I supposed to do? My beef ain't with that nigga anyway. I want his precious son," I told her, feeling the rage boil inside me to the point I felt its heat in my mouth.

"DJ was raised by the man I just described. What should you do? Use caution! Your mother went up against him unprepared, and I just don't wanna lose you, Tae," she whispered, tears spilling down her face.

Her old eyes carried so much wisdom, but that wisdom came from the pain of experience. I'd always felt like she knew what happened to my mom, but whenever I approached the topic she shut down.

"No disrespect, Ms. Gladys, but we gotta handle this ourselves. I get that this is a touchy situation, and it's family involved, but the streets is watching. Heads gotta come off, plain and simple," Ruby said, gripping my hand tighter.

"Tae, please, you've just had major knee surgery to replace your knee cap completely! You're in no condition for this, baby," she pleaded, still crying.

"My woman and child are helpless and innocent in all this. I've got no choice, Grandma."

I could tell she knew arguing was a waste of time, and with no more words to speak, she stood up. "I'll get you discharged from the hospital. And I'll be praying for you both," she told us, walking out of the room.

"Can you walk?" Ruby asked, laying her head on my shoulder.

"I don't know. I haven't been awake long enough to try. All this dope they got me on has me feeling sick as shit, but I'm not feeling the full extent of the pain like I was."

"Why would you travel without me, Tae? Come on, homie, you know better than to do some dumb shit like that."

"I know. We just wanted to spend some time alone."

I knew that statement would cause her to go silent. She knew what my relationship was, but the reality was every relationship had its issues. Ruby was my best friend, so we talked about everything. And when the time for words ran out, we fucked occasionally, too. It wouldn't affect our friendship because we wouldn't let it, but at times like this it did make it difficult.

"I'm sorry, Chantel!"

"Don't call me that, boy, you know I hate that shit," she said, elbowing me lightly.

"This shit could get ugly, ma. You ready for that?" I asked, looking at her.

When she looked up, I saw something I rarely did: there were tears swimming in those big, brown eyes. Before I could utter a word, she kissed me hard, forcing her tongue between my dry lips until all I tasted was the trademark Coca-Cola Slurpee she was forever drinking. The drugs had me hazy, but I knew what that was. I just couldn't believe she'd do this now.

"Ruby, hold up!" I told her, pulling back. She didn't try to kiss me again, but instead began to wiggle out of her jeans. "Ruby, don't do that!"

"Shut up, Tae. I know exactly how ugly shit will get going up against Devaughn Mitchell and his "family." I need this now, just in case."

I didn't get a chance to respond before she was gently pulling my covers back, lifting my gown, and guiding her naked bottom half down on my hard dick. Obviously my body had a mind of its own, because I had no idea I'd gotten hard. She only weighed about 120 pounds, so I took her weight without a problem as she inched her way down my dick. Her pussy was so tight and wet that I almost forgot to breathe once I was completely buried inside her.

"Look at me, Tae," she ordered, taking my hands in hers, slowly going up and down.

I saw our entire history in her eyes. I saw us smoking our first blunt, jumping our first crip. I saw us catching our first body, and the first time I'd seen her body naked. Even though her build was slight with her small titties and little round booty, she still had some of the tightest pussy I'd ever been in.

"Shit, Ruby, you're gonna make me cum, I panted as she began moving faster and swirling her hips.

"Look at me, baby," she replied, bringing her face inches from my own.

It seemed like we were breathing as one, and the taste of her was so sweet. My hands found their way to her hips and I lifted her higher, feeling her cum in a rush as my dick fought its way deeper into her despite the screaming pain in my knee. Before I wanted to, I felt my cum shooting inside of her, and I bit her bottom lip to keep from screaming out.

She didn't move until she felt the steady stream of hotness stop spewing in her. I could taste her blood in my mouth as she kissed me one last time before rolling off me and putting her clothes back on. There was a heavy silence that filled the room following our quickie, and I wasn't sure how to fill it. Our sex had never been that intense, and we'd never done it without protection before. Words were needed.

"Chantel, I—"

"Nah, homie, we not doing this right now. It's time to put our game face on and get it poppin', dig me?"

I knew she was right, but I also knew she was frontin'. I wouldn't push, though, so I simply shook my head and tried to swing my legs over the edge of the bed.

Aryanna

Chapter 7

2040

Before my feet could touch the ground, a nurse was coming through the door with a wheelchair. The knowing smile she gave me that went from her brightly-painted red lips to her sparkling blue eyes told me the smell of sex was in the air. I felt relief that it wasn't my grandmother.

"Mr. Briggs, you shouldn't try to walk just yet. You need to give yourself time," the nurse said, pushing the wheelchair right up against the bed.

"I gotta get out of here, so it's no time like the present to see if my knee will hold," I replied, sliding slowly from the bed until my feet were firmly on the floor.

"Lean against me," she said, stepping to my side and putting my arm around her neck.

She smelled sweet, like fresh flowers with a hint of cinnamon, and her body was deceptively firm beneath her uniform. I was hesitant to lean all 215 pounds of my 6'3" frame on her, but she felt like she could take it despite the size difference. She couldn't have been more than 5'9", maybe weighing 160 pounds, but she held up under the pressure as I took my tentative first step.

The pain was swift, immediately snatching my breath away, but the thought of Brianna and my baby pushed me to keep going. The only upside was that he'd shot me in my left knee, which meant I could drive still.

"Take it easy," the nurse said, guiding me slowly around the foot of the bed.

By now Ruby was relaxing, but the look on her face was one of anger. She wasn't directing that look at me, though.

"That's it, sweetheart, one step at a time," the nurse encouraged, still walking with me.

I heard her, but my eyes were locked on Ruby, who was now sliding off the bed. "Ruby."

"I got it, nurse. I can help him work his knee out," she said, coming to my other side.

"Well, I really should be the one."

"Listen, ma, what you really should do is walk away. The pussy you smell in the air? Yeah, that's mine, which means the dick is spoken for. So I'ma kindly suggest you take your bleach-blonde, thirsty ass on somewhere, because this is as nice as I'ma say it."

All I could do was shake my head as the nurse quickly released her hold on me and hauled ass out the door. "Your ass is crazy!" I told her, laughing.

"What I say?" she asked with the best innocent smile she could manage.

Before the door could close good on the nurse's exit, a man I assumed was my doctor came through it. "Mr. Briggs, I'm Dr. Mathis. How are you holding up?"

"You tell me, Doc. I mean, how bad was it?" I asked, taking a seat back on the bed so he could examine me.

"Well, the bullet shattered your knee cap, so we had to replace it. We used a titanium alloy that still allows you to move freely, so you don't have to worry about any lasting limitations. You will, of course, experience some pain and discomfort, but ultimately you'll heal just fine. Luckily for you, this type of surgery is more common nowadays, and the medical field has made vast improvements. You'll move like new by tomorrow," he replied, straightening my leg out and massaging behind my knee.

"Ok, so am I discharged?"

"All you have to do is sign a few forms and you're good to go. I will warn you that the police were waiting to question you and are speaking with your grandma now."

"Thanks for the heads up," I told him, standing again so Ruby could help me get dressed. The doctor left, and we quickly put my clothes on. "You got a pistol?" I asked, climbing into the wheelchair the nurse left me.

"You know I do," she replied, stepping behind the wheelchair and pushing me toward the door.

As soon as I was wheeled through the door, we came face-to-face with the cops the doctor had warned me about, but he had neglected to mention they weren't regular police.

"Mr. Briggs, my name is Special Agent McDonald, and this is my partner, Agent Kelly. We need to ask you a few questions about the shooting and kidnapping that took place."

"I would love to be of some assistance, but as you can see I'm recovering from a gunshot wound," I replied, gesturing toward my left knee.

"Considering the video footage of your pregnant girlfriend and you entering the mall tells us who was kidnapped, because it's obvious she's not here now, I would think you would be eager to help us learn her whereabouts. Unless you already know?" Agent Kelly said with a questioning and suspicious look on her face.

I had always been taught that we don't talk to the cops, but I knew exceptions were made because we had them on the payroll. But this was the FBI, the watchers of the watchers, and under no circumstances were we to talk to them.

"I don't know where Brianna is or why she was taken. What I do know is that you're wasting time here questioning me when you could be looking for her," I told them, hoping my face didn't give away all the emotions I was feeling beneath the surface.

"We are doing our job, but your closed-mouth, code-of-the-streets mentality is only hurting us and slowing us down. Agent Kelly and I are the best at what we do, and since this is being investigated as an act of domestic terrorism, we will bring the whole force of the FBI down on those responsible. And anyone who stands in our way," he said, giving me a pointed look.

"Let's go," I told Ruby, and we left the agents standing there with my grandmother. As soon as we were out of earshot, I began issuing orders. "I want the video footage from the mall A.S.A.P. I want our people to find out everything they can about my brother, as well as my father, but they need to do it quietly because the streets talk. Lastly, I want a sit down with the big homies as soon as you can arrange it. And I want you there with me."

"Where else would I be, my dude? It's 'til the casket drops with me and you, always has been, and don't nothing change that," she replied seriously.

Words couldn't express how much I needed her right now. This was the world, winner-take-all, and there was no way I could lose anymore.

Chapter 8

Deshana

2027

I never imagined anything could hurt me this much, even after living through the hell of losing my daddy, but I was wrong. It was taking everything in my power to keep the screaming in my head down to a frenzied panic, but only God knew how long I could maintain before I blacked out again. I knew I'd blacked out because I was missing pieces of time from my memory. If only I could forget seeing my sister's head in that box, or erase the knowledge of who put it there.

Laying on the cold marble floor in a pool of my own vomit, my brain still screamed out *why?* Because I didn't understand how the man I loved came to harm my own flesh and blood. It didn't make sense. Nothing made sense!

I felt her arms around me before I heard her voice. "Come on, sis, we gotta pull it together," JuJu said, holding my head in her lap and rocking me gently like La-La had when I was a kid. The fresh wave of tears almost choked me, but I was powerless to stop their flood. At this point I felt I could cry for the rest of my life. I knew with absolute certainty what I was feeling would be with me always. The void, anger, loss, and torment would never go away.

"Why, JuJu? Why her?"

"I don't know, sweetheart, I really don't. But I promise you will get that answer before we end his miserable fucking life!" she replied, holding me tighter. "Come on, let's get you up off the floor and cleaned up."

I allowed her to pull me to my feet, and I noticed for the first time I was covered in blood. I could feel my entire body shaking as my mind fought to get some type of understanding and grip on reality. I knew I hadn't picked up anything out of that box, so who's blood was on me? Because my own from the gunfight had dried already. "JuJu? I'm-I'm covered in fresh blood. Whose is it?"

As hazy and disoriented as my thoughts were, I could still see the look of concern she was giving me. "You don't remember?"

My response was to slowly shaking my head and hope I hadn't done anything worth regretting.

Before she could answer, we both spun around as the front door opened, and in stumbled a blast from the past. "Is that?" JuJu asked in a whisper, grabbing my hand to steady me.

"Yeah. It is," I replied as my father came through the door behind Keyz. I didn't get a chance to say anything before he smacked her across the back of her head with the butt of his pistol, and she came sliding across the floor, stopping only inches from my feet.

"Where?" he asked, heading straight for the panic room after JuJu nodded her head. It took only a moment before I felt his roar rumbling off the walls of the house in rage and pain. The sound of his soul bleeding sent a chill down my spine, but it also warmed my heart because I knew those responsible would pay with their lives.

Her asking me what happened refocused my attention on the open front door where my grandmother stood. "La-La. La-La is dead, Nana," I told her, tasting the throw up in my mouth at just having to speak that truth out loud.

It wasn't until then I noticed the man with his hand on my grandmother's arm. "Why are you holding her? Don't you know who that is? I suggest you take your damn hands off my grandma before my father comes back out," I warned.

"He knows," the guard told me.

"He knows? Dad, what's going on?" I asked, bewildered. "Later for that," my grandmother replied. Something in her eyes told me this story could only end badly, but I didn't understand how. My grandmother being man-handled made even less sense than my sister being dead.

"Get them down to the basement," my father ordered, coming out of the panic room carrying the box. One of the soldiers scooped up Keyz while the other marched my grandma to the waiting elevator.

"Dad, talk to me," I pleaded, trailing behind him while still clutching JuJu's hand. He didn't respond, but he didn't try to stop me from getting on the elevator with him. For a brief moment I was able to look into his eyes, and what I saw terrified me. I'd seen him kill before, seen the look on his face in that moment of long-awaited satisfaction. But what I saw now I couldn't put into words. The light was gone from his eyes, almost as if his soul no longer existed. What I saw in that moment was *nothing*.

Our destination was no surprise to me once the elevator came to a stop, but when we entered the room, my baby sister's butchered body was a surprise that made me freeze at the doors. "JuJu?" I whispered, hoping for some type of explanation that I could live with.

Jordyn was laying on the cold metal table with visible stab wounds to at least ninety percent of her body. And if that wasn't bad enough, her head had been severed as well. The knife was still in her chest, almost as if the work wasn't finished and it was simply waiting for the owner's return.

My father absorbed the sight without a word, and then turned around to us for an explanation. "I-I-I, um."

"Breath, Deshana. Just breathe and tell me what happened," he encouraged.

"I don't think she remembers, sir," JuJu said, which caused me to look at her for an explanation, too. "After the box, when the phone went dead, it was because I was chasing after Deshana. Something in her just snapped, and she came down here and, well, you see," she concluded, gesturing toward the body on the table.

I hadn't forgotten what Jordyn did to me by siding with Keyz or by shooting me, but the rage I'd unleashed on her was way more than that. Now wasn't the time to analyze what it was, but I knew my memories of this moment would be long to fade.

"Get her off the table and dispose of her body," my father said to one of the soldiers. The one who was closest was the one holding Keyz, so he laid her on the ground and enlisted the help of another to get the remains of Jordyn.

"Dad, talk to me," I pleaded, finally stepping into the room.

"Ramona. Ramona got shot in the throat. I don't know how bad it is, but your sister is at the hospital with her right now. I got there too late to stop her from going after Keyz, and now she might die for the mistakes I've made," he said in a voice hollow and haunted with his worst fears.

"She will pull through, Dad. She's a fighter, and she has so much to live for. And now that you've got Keyz, the war is over, and you can make her pay for shooting Ramona on top of everything else."

"She didn't shoot Ramona. My own mother did," he said, shaking his head in obvious disbelief and pain.

The words I was prepared to speak stuck in my throat. What could I say to that? I had no idea the torment and anguish he was feeling, not to mention the indecision of what his next move would be.

"I didn't mean to shoot her, son. I had no idea who Kiara was fighting, and had I known, you know I would have stopped it. I'm so sorry," she said, tears clouding her eyes before spilling over onto her cheeks.

"Explain to me how you came to be on Kiara's side at all, considering she's the one who shot me in the first place."

I could tell by the look on her face this was new information to her and made her feel a lot worse. "She-she came by my house and dropped her son off, asking me to keep him safe. One look at that little boy and I knew he was yours. It didn't matter how or why you'd slept with your sister, all I knew was I had to protect my grandbaby the way I never protected you."

"Son? She has a son?"

"Yes, and the baby, he looks every bit like you did at that age. I didn't know anything about her shooting you. I mean, nobody tells me shit. All I knew was you died, and that's the pain I've been carrying for the last five years."

I saw him weighing her words as he would a stranger, and that told me just how close he was to killing his own mother. For the first time in my life, I actually feared my father and what he was capable of. For the first time, I saw a man I didn't know at all.

Aryanna

Chapter 9

2027

"Keyz was the one who shot me and tried to end my life. Her son is my son, but she fucked me in my sleep in order to have him. She was obsessed with me, and in the end that shit drove her to her breaking point. I've been in a coma for the last five years, hidden away and cared for by the woman you just shot. I'm telling you all this, Mom, so you can understand just how big of a miscalculation you made. Because if Ramona dies, so do you," he told her coldly.

No one in the room doubted his sincerity, nor did they question his judgment. If we had all learned one thing, it was that you didn't cross Devaughn Mitchell. No one was safe when you did that.

"You can say that to me, son? Your own mother?" she asked in disbelief.

"I'm a man of my word, so I suggest you spend less time questioning what I said and focus more on praying for your life."

We were all so focused on this exchanged that no one had been paying attention to Keyz, who had regained consciousness. As quick as a cat, she was off the floor and running full speed into JuJu, knocking her off balance. Her attack was so sudden it even took the soldiers by surprise, and she was able to knock two of them over. Helping JuJu up, I leapt into action, grabbing the fallen soldier's mac-11 and chasing the shadow of Keyz down the hall toward the stairs.

"Get that bitch," I heard my father yell from behind me, hot on my heels.

I let the mac spray even though I knew I couldn't hit her, hoping my shots could defy the laws of gravity. My rational mind told me not to rush around the corner of the stairs because it was a blind spot she could be lying in, but at this point I couldn't give a fuck about caution. I rounded the corner still letting the mac bark, but she wasn't there, so I took the stairs two at a time in pursuit. I could hear her footsteps not too far off in the distance, and then I heard gunfire rumble through the house.

Coming off the stairs into the foyer I saw two bodies laying on the floor and a man's silhouette standing in the doorway. "Who the fuck are you?" I screamed, upping the mac immediately and preparing to squeeze the trigger.

"Devaughn sent me," he replied, obviously smart enough to keep his gun at his side.

I caught sight of JuJu in my peripheral vision, and only then did I move forward until I was standing over the bodies. Keyz moaned in pain, but was still attempting to crawl to the gun that had been knocked from her grip when she was hit. I kicked her in her face for good measure, knocking her unconscious as well as sending two of her teeth scattering across the floor. JuJu still had her gun on the dude standing by the door, and she was ordering him to put his gun down. He complied and walked toward us with his hands by his side in a non-threatening manner.

"It's okay, that's a homie, 6'9"," my dad said, coming up behind me.

"That's your homie?" I told him, and he could see we were serious because neither me nor JuJu lowered our guns.

I heard my father's gun clatter to the floor as he made his way to the second body on the floor. I could tell who it was even in the dim light, and my heart hurt for this woman I loved.

Without a word, he knelt beside Candy and pulled what was left of her ruined head into his lap. There was no question of life left. The neat bullet hole and the fact she was missing the back of her head told the story. Our lack of attention had allowed Keyz to take one more loved one from our life.

I'd never heard my father cry before. I had always assumed he just didn't know how. But in this moment all his pain finally gave way to wails of such complete sorrow I feared the world would know and hear his misery. I laid my gun down and took a step toward him to offer whatever comfort I could.

It was only then I noticed the presence and felt the heat of someone staring at me. I looked at him and he looked back, his eyes so full of naked pain and understanding far superior to his years.

"Who shot Mommy, Daddy?"

Aryanna

Chapter 10

DJ

2040

If I actually had time to pull over or form a coherent thought, I might've kept good on my promise to gag her. The wonders of childbirth always amazed me, but the sound of her pain was enough to make me respect the opposite sex who had to go through the miracle.

"I need a hospital!" she screamed in between her breathing exercises. That was probably the understatement of a lifetime, because she needed a few hospitals and their staff if her screams and the liquid in my front seat were any indications.

I almost lost control of the car as I rounded the corner into our driveway, but at the last moment the tires grabbed traction and my horsepower allowed me to gallop to safety. We flew past the main house, which loomed ominously in its black glass and silver paneling against the midday sky. The odds were better than good my father would be alerted of my return, but I had bigger problems to worry about.

Screeching to a stop in my garage, I ordered the door shut and had the intercom page Coco to my location. "Don't worry, I've got the best help that money can buy," I told her, coming around to the passenger side of the car to help her out.

At first she was reluctant to take my hand, which was understandable given the fact I'd kidnapped her, but she eventually realized her options were slim. I helped her into the living room just as Coco reached the bottom of the stairs.

"What the fuck? DJ, why is there a chick about to deliver a baby on your couch?" she asked, both wonder and jealousy coating her words.

"It's a long story, and now ain't the time for it. I need your help because I have no idea what I'm doing."

"Why didn't you just take her to the hospital then? Why bring her here?"

"Enough with the damn questions, Courtney! Either help me and bring me some fucking towels or take your ass home!" I yelled. I knew I was being harsh because her questions were good ones, no more than anyone else would ask in this situation. Now just wasn't the time, though.

My tone galvanized her into gear, and she took to the stairs like a hurdler.

"DJ? DJ, where you at?" I heard my father call, coming through my front door.

I didn't even have time to respond or fear what may be coming because my hand was suddenly in vise grip as another contraction ripped through her.

In that moment it struck me as weird that I didn't know her name.

"You're gonna break my hand, bitch!"

"Fuck! Fuck you, nigga, this shit is your fucking fault, so the least you can do is hold my hand!" she yelled right back at me, sweat rolling off her forehead and down into the pool it was making on my white leather sofa.

I couldn't argue that. This may have been my fault, so I did have to see this through with her. But damn, did she have to be so strong?

Coco came back with the towels at the exact moment my father entered the living room. I saw him give her that *what the fuck* look, but all she did was shake her head and hand me the towels. I didn't know what to do with them, I just knew every movie I'd ever seen involving childbirth made it out to be a very messy thing.

"DJ, who is this, and why the hell is she getting ready to give birth in this house?" my father asked in what passed for his calm voice. I knew he wasn't calm, though. Oh no, he was pissed!

"It's a long story, Dad."

"Make it a short one, and it better make damn good sense," he replied, standing close enough to me for me to feel his anger filling the air.

At that moment I was saved by a contraction intense enough to rip the average woman in half. I thought she might levitate off the couch, but she rode the storm like this was her life's work before collapsing back into the puddle of her own sweat. I didn't know much about childbirth in general, but I knew the faster her contractions came meant the faster the baby was coming.

"I asked you a question, son."

"And I don't have an answer, Dad. At least not one you're gonna like."

"It doesn't matter how little I like it at this point because this baby is coming regardless. If it's yours, we—"

"It's not his baby!" she panted through her breathing exercises.

"Then why are you here?" my father asked logically.

"Kidnapped," she blurted out just as her next contraction hit hard.

"Dad."

"Shut up! I wanna hear what she has to say, because it's obviously something you're trying to hide."

The room was silent for a moment except for her labored breathing and my heart beating loudly in my ears. "He-he kidnapped me and shot my baby's father," she managed to get out once the pain had subsided.

"I'm sorry, would you like to repeat that statement?" my father said slowly, obviously wishing he had heard her wrong. "You. You better answer my goddamn question before I put my hands on you," he warned me in that deadly whisper he was infamous for.

How could I explain this? What words would justify a war he had no idea about? And to top it off, it was his son involved. Granted he didn't claim Devonte, but he was still the product of his seed, and that might mean something.

"The simplest way to explain this is to tell you who her baby's father is. She's having a baby by Devonte."

"Devonte? You mean you shot your own brother and kidnapped his girlfriend?" my father roared, stepping right up next to me so I could feel the heat from his breath.

"Your brother?" both Coco and Brianna exclaimed at the same time.

"Boy, have you lost your fucking mind or did you just leave it at school?" he asked, smacking me upside my head.

"Dad I-I can explain."

"And you damn well will, but right now we have got to save my grandbaby. I'm going to call, Kristi and she will help with the delivery. Until she gets here, you better not leave her side, understand?"

"Yes, sir."

"Brianna, you're gonna be fine, sweetheart. Just keep doing what you were taught in your classes."

"How-how do you know my name?" she asked in between contractions, which caused me to finally look at my father with the same question swimming in my eyes.

"Just because you don't see me don't mean I not keeping tabs on you and Tae," he replied, avoiding my glance. I never knew he cared enough about his illegitimate son to actually keep an eye on him, but I guess there was a lot I didn't know about my father.

"Courtney, it's time for you to go," he told her, leading her by her hand to the door. I heard the door close behind them, and then it was just me and her. And the baby screaming to get out.

"This baby is coming! I'm not ready for it yet!" she screamed in panic.

Shit, if she wasn't ready, then how in the hell did she think I felt? One thing I did know was there weren't any do-overs, so if that little person was ready to come, then shit had just got realer.

"Ok, um, it'll be ok. I'm not going anywhere," I told her, moving around until I was in between her spread legs. Thank God she was wearing a dress, because taking her clothes off would have made this just that much more awkward.

"Oh god, oh god, I can't have my daughter like this! Not with you and not like this! Please get someone to help me before it's too late!" she pleaded, tears now mixing with the sweat and joining the puddle she was lying in.

"There is no one else. Listen, not matter what drama Devonte and I have, I promise I won't hurt your baby or you."

"You're lying! You-you kidnapped me, and now you've forced my baby to come early!" she wailed, her cries starting to take on an edge of hysteria.

"I know what I did, and I'm sorry, but I'm here with you and we have to do this together, so calm down. Whether we like it or not, that baby is coming," I told her, really getting a look at her pussy. Unless I missed an important part about the female anatomy in health class, there was the top of a head stretching her beyond my wildest dreams. This was the scariest and most fascinating moment of my life, and I prayed the fear wouldn't win out and have me passed the fuck out in the next minute.

"*Ahh!*" Her screams seemed to rock my whole house, and they definitely shook me to my foundation. All I could do was look on in complete amazement as her pussy steadily got wider and the hair that marked her landing strip suddenly became a whole bush.

"She's coming! I can see her head!"

"No shit, asshole, I can feel it!" she replied, breathing so fast I thought she might pass out her damn self.

"Push!" I coached.

"Tell m-me something I do-don't know!" she growled back.

"Um, well, your pussy is still pretty, even with a head sticking out."

The look she gave me at that comment was most certainly a kill shot if that feat were possible. It made me smile, though. That smile quickly faded when I realized this magic show was not over. Just when I thought I was amazed, I became even more so with the fact her pussy could stretch even further. I'd heard the head wasn't the difficult part of the birthing process, it was those shoulders. Granted I'd never slept with this girl, but her pussy looked extremely tight before all hell broke loose. I didn't see how this baby was coming out of this hole.

Her screams took on a baritone the likes of which I'd never heard, and then before I had time to realize what was happening, I was holding her little girl in my hands. She was beautiful, so tiny and just beautiful! I'd never seen a more perfect woman in my life, but there was one problem.

"DJ? DJ, why isn't she crying?"

Chapter 11

2040

"DJ! Answer me! Why isn't she crying?

I may not have known much, but I knew this was a true statement. I also knew that as this little girl's mother, she was now caught in the throws of a parent's worst nightmare. I couldn't feel her little heart beating, and when I checked she wasn't breathing at all. I felt panic wanting to seize control of my body, but my brain was fighting it off while it searched for ways to fix this situation.

The only experience I had with CPR stemmed from time spent at my father's boys' and girls' clubs during the summers, but this little baby in my hands was entirely too small for me to put the weight of my body on her chest.

"DJ!" Brianna screamed, the look in her eyes telling me panic had officially moved in and taken up residence in every part of her body.

Remembering something I'd seen on YouTube years ago, I immediately scooped the amniotic fluid out of the baby's mouth with my pinky to make sure its airway was clear, then I turned the baby around in my arms until I could hold her with my hands wrapped around her upper body. Once I had her where I could support her head and still get my hands around her, I gently began squeezing her in the rhythm of a heartbeat.

By now Brianna was screaming her head off and crying, but I drown all that out as I kept up with the steady compressions to my niece's chest. Just as I was about to give her over to fate, she coughed a little before drawing in the biggest breath her tiny body could muster.

The next sounds that filled the room were the sweetest I'd ever heard in my entire life as she started wailing her little head off at the injustice of not being in the safety of her mother's womb.

"My baby! Give me my baby!" she cried, opening her arms wide and letting tears of joy replace those of sorrow that had just filled her. I did as she said, only too happy to be able to give her that beautiful bundle of joy instead of a pain that would never leave.

It wasn't until then I noticed her pussy was still leaking, and something that resembled old liver had landed on my couch. On the white leather this whole ordeal looked like a murder scene, but it felt better to have saved this life than taken it.

I heard the front door open behind me and two sets of footsteps walking toward us.

"I brought help," my dad said, proceeding to bring Kristi into the room. Kristi had been my grandfather's wife at one point in life, but she was never a stepparent to my dad. They had a weird friendship going back to even before I was born, but one thing was for certain, and that was their loyalty to each other. Whenever my dad called, she came, and it was vice versa. She was one of the few people he trusted, and in times like this I was glad she was on the team, because she was a career ER nurse.

"I need to examine her," Kristi said, reaching for the little girl, but Brianna wouldn't turn her loose.

Kristi looked at my dad, who in turn looked at me. I don't know what type of sway he thought I had, but given what had just happened, I didn't think Jesus could pry that child from her arms.

"Brianna? Brianna, just let her make sure she's alright. I promise she won't hurt her, and she's the best nurse we know."

At first she just looked at me and then down at her precious baby girl, now napping peacefully in her mother's arms. When she looked back at me, I could still see the distrust in her eyes, but I could also see the gratitude for all I had done during the crisis we had faced.

Slowly, reluctantly she handed the baby to Kristi, who immediately began a thorough check of the baby from her head to her tiny little toes.

"Were there any complications during birth?" Kristi asked.

Again Brianna looked at me, but this time I understood she couldn't speak the words of what we had to endure. I filled Kristi in while my father listened, recounting everything that had happened.

Once that was complete, Kristi went back to checking the baby, and eventually moved on to checking Brianna. While that was going on, my father pulled me into the hall where he could take a chunk out of my ass in private.

"Start talking," he said as soon as we were out of ear shot.

"I made a move against Devonte."

He was smart enough not to ask why. I was pretty sure he remembered all the late nights he had to hold me and console me after my mother's death. He may have kept her killer's identity a secret at first, but nothing in the dark stays there long. Since I couldn't make my aunt Keyz pay, her son would just have to do it.

"Why now, DJ? Why fuck up your whole life by trying to take it to the streets? You ain't a street nigga, son. You're a school boy, and I wanted you that way. The streets don't offer shit except misguided loyalty and death. You wanna die?"

"I'm not as square as you think, pops, so who's to say that I'ma be the one that wakes up dead? Do you really think that

I went away to school for one kind of education?" I asked him seriously.

I could see him weighing things out rapidly in his mind, but transparent wasn't a word I would use to describe it in the slightest. "So now you think you're street smart, huh? Boy, you're eighteen fucking years old! You ain't even learned how to fuck good yet," he said, laughing in my face.

I wanted to be disrespectful, but I knew that wasn't an option. Besides, actions spoke louder than words. "Let me show you something real quick," I told him, turning and leading the way to my office through my living room. It was time to show my father exactly who his son was.

I placed my palm on the scanner and stepped inside once the door was open. "Lights on, computer systems on, security code word Judas." My orders were followed and my base of operations came to life under the watchful gaze of my father.

The room was thirty-by-thirty with wall-to-wall black carpet. There were three different computers sitting on top of my massive maple wood desk against the far wall, giving me a clear view of anyone entering the room. There were two low-backed leather chairs sitting in front of my desk, and I offered one to my father now as I took my seat in front of the computer monitors.

"What is all of this?" he asked, trying to hide the surprise I knew I detected in his voice.

"My office, and my home away from home. You may not approve of everything I'm about to tell you, but I would appreciate if you would listen with an open mind."

My request was met with silence, but he didn't dismiss me out of hand, so I continued.

"You sent me to school to get an education, and I did, and you know this based on my grades as well as my graduation. I met a lot of interesting people while I was in school, and I feel like that was part of your plan, too. You taught me a long time ago that my friends will be politicians. Some will own fortune five hundred companies. My point is that I've formed friendships, partnerships, and business relationships without using your connections. For whatever reason, you've always left the drug game alone, even though it had a part to do with how you started making money. I saw just how big and how high the drug game reaches while I was in school. And it's a lot of untapped revenue, Dad. I'm not talking about owning street corners or doing shit that was done way before my time. I'm speaking more toward the smarter side of the drug trade, because we both know the dealer don't make even a third of the money the supplier makes."

I paused in my speech to bring up the software prototype that allowed for face-time conversations in 3D. "I put together a team of just a few people from school I felt had the same vision as me, and we went into business for ourselves. As you know, synthetic drugs have been the wave of my generation, mainly because it's easier to beat a piss test and because the prison sentences aren't as harsh.

"There was a girl I met at school named Harley, and she's a fucking genius when it comes to chemistry and what's necessary to create the most powerful drugs that you can't test for. The problem was that she was a pimp's whore, and she couldn't get out of that situation on her own. She came from a long line of whores out of West Virginia, so that was basically all she knew besides her book smarts. I put her on the team, and we came up with a synthetic form of every mainstream drug on the market. From there we distributed in mass quantities throughout the world, mainly aligning ourselves with whatever form of organized crime operating in that hemisphere. Pops, this shit is gold! I have over $300,000,000 of my own money right now, and I made that in no time."

"Explain to me what this has to do with your brother, and why now?" he said, still maintaining a neutral expression.

"Money and power don't make me whole, nor do they make me happy. You of all people should understand that," I said.

"Son, I understand you wanting revenge for what happened to your mother, and trust me there's not a day that goes by when I don't want the same. But the reality is we don't always get what we want. Sometimes sacrifices are needed in order for the overall picture to make sense."

"What do you mean? No sacrifice is worth my mother's death going unanswered. To you she may have just been a side piece, but—"

"Watch your mouth, and remember who you are talking to," he warned, the fire I'd heard so much about coming to life in his eyes.

"This is my mother we're talking about. Do you know what it's like growing up without a mother?"

"I do. I never told you that your grandma – hell, the majority of your family – have been junkies my whole life. Junkies make lousy parents and relatives. So yes, son, I know what it's like to grow up without a mother. I was raised by the streets, and I saw things that still make me cringe to this day. I come from a generation where if someone in your immediate family wasn't a crackhead, we didn't have anything in common. I come from a generation when food stamps were still coming in paper form that were multicolored. You ever had to use food stamps, DJ?"

"No, sir."

"Exactly, because I have always provided the best for you, even when I was in a coma. And you may not have had your biological mother with you your whole life, but you still had a woman's love and guidance. Now you have the nerve to come to me like you are some kingpin? Get real, nigga. You just got an acceptance letter from Tulane University in New Orleans today, and you think I'ma let you throw all that away? You got me fucked up!" he barked savagely, the calm look he'd been projecting now long gone and forgotten.

"With all due respect, pops, you got me fucked up if you think I'ma let this go."

I saw the flash in his eyes at the realization of what my words meant, but I wouldn't back down, not from him or anyone else who stood in my way when it came to exacting revenge for my mother.

"Boy, do you know what I've sacrificed for you? And now—"

Before he could finish his sentence, the link alerting me to an incoming message from The Mad Hacker went off. "Talk to me, Evy," I said once his 3D image popped up next to my computer monitor.

"We got a big fucking problem, DJ! Harley was found dead a little while ago, and it wasn't from natural causes." I could feel the heat of my father's stare, but I kept focusing on what I was being told. "Her body was found burned to a crisp, but her I.D. was left at the scene because whoever did it wanted her identified A.S.A.P. But there's more: she was burned to death inside a warehouse your dad owns in Virginia."

At this revelation I looked at my dad, and the look on his face surprised me. "Dad?"

"They're coming," he replied.

"Who?" I asked.

"You started a war, son. I hope you're ready for this, because you just woke a fucking sleeping giant."

Aryanna

Chapter 12

Kevin

2027

The knowledge that my sworn enemy was still alive changed the game dramatically. His family would still pay for all he had done, but now he would have to live with that truth as well until it came time for him to meet his end. Killing Latavia and taking her chopped-off head to his doorstep was just the beginning.

"What's our next move, son?" my mother asked as we stood outside of our old apartment building.

"Well, now they know we are her, but they may not know who we are yet. That's our edge, along with the fact we know Devaughn is still alive. What hurts us is we don't know where he is or any other vital information that could help with regards to his weaknesses. His daughter's death is gonna send him into a blind fury, and we can use that to our advantage, because he will come to us once he figures our identity out."

"Maybe him knowing who we are is not such a good idea."

Her tone caused me to look closer at her, willing my vision to penetrate the night's gloom and read her true expression in this moment. "What do you mean? What's wrong, Mom?" I asked, taking her hand in my own. Her fingers were cool to the touch, which was unlike her.

"You know I knew your father for many years. We went through a lot together. I saw multiple sides of Timmy, and no matter how bad it got, I still loved him the same through whatever. There was only one time I ever saw him unsure and afraid. That was when he realized he had to go head-to-head with Devaughn Mitchell. Your father wasn't always a nice man, and he could be cold-hearted when he had to be, but Devaughn was an enemy unlike anyone he had faced before, and that worried him. There were times he expressed to me his regret at trying to have Devaughn killed, but he said it was a necessary move in the moment. But how could you face a man that was too evil to die?

"I thought he was exaggerating and making this man seem like a boogie man, but now that I know he's alive, I'm starting to believe he really may be the devil in disguise."

I took in her words and let them bounce around my head in silence. This was a lot of information to process, because it didn't fit with what I knew of my father. I mean, the man seemed ten feet tall and fearless, but here my own mother stood telling me he was afraid of a mere man. What I wanted to know was if it was simply paranoia, or did my father have a right to fear this man?

"Mom, there's no going back at this point, and even if we could, I wouldn't. This man killed my father, and he has to answer for that. And he's gonna answer to me," I told her with steel determination. I felt her squeeze my hand, but I didn't know if it was reassurance or her own fear that caused the movement.

"Then we do this together, son. So what's our next move going to be?"

This was a very good question. Some of our advantages had been taken, but not all of it, and now was the time to seize what was left. Pulling my phone from my pocket, I placed a call that would put the next piece in this chess match into my clutches.

"This is Trey," I said when the phone was answered.

"I'm here, sir," she replied.

"Do it!" I told her before disconnecting the call and putting the phone away.

"Who was that, Kevin?" my mother asked.

"Just someone who works for us. I just had Devaughn's ex-wife, and the mother to his kids, taken from St. Elizabeth's mental institution, where she's been for the last five years. She's being taken to Norfolk, and we will continue to wage this war from there."

In my opinion, it was best to be on familiar ground considering the fact we now knew Devaughn was alive. This thought gave me a flash of brilliance as another plan began to formulate in my mind. No one knew he was alive, but I bet a lot of people would find that interesting. Pulling my phone back out, I made another quick call.

"Heart foundation."

"This is Holford for Murdaheart," I said.

"One moment, please."

If I played this right, then I would have to do little more than pick up the pieces, or pick the bones clean of rotting corpses others would leave.

"I see you've been a busy boy, Kev," he said by way of answering the phone.

"Indeed I have, and since you've been so instrumental in all of my success, I thought I would throw you a bone."

"Oh yeah? Well, throw the dog a bone, homie."

I wanted to tell him I wasn't his goddamn homie, but I saw no reason to provoke someone who would prove useful to me and my cause. "I thought some people would be very interested to know that a certain someone ain't dead."

"Oh yeah? And who would that undead individual be?"

"Devaughn Mitchell."

My revelation was immediately met with a very loud silence, almost the same one that had seemed to choke my mother a short time ago. "Murdaheart, did you hear me?" I asked, wondering if we'd been disconnected. I knew

Murdaheart wasn't scared. I mean, he was a leader in the Blood movement, too, which had to put him on the same level as Devaughn.

"He's-he's not dead? Who told you a lie like that?" he asked, a slight tremble filling his voice and causing just a tiny bit of unease to creep over me.

"His daughter told me before she died."

"Wait, this nigga is alive, and you killed his daughter?"

Now his tone of voice had me rethinking the wisdom in my decision to make this call. He sounded like I said I was Judas and had betrayed Jesus or something. "Yeah, and?"

"And? And, nigga, you better get the fuck out of dodge and quick, because you don't even wanna know how bad this is about to get for you."

"Me? Don't you mean how bad it's about to get for us? I know you don't think the nigga you all are so afraid of is going to overlook the fact a lot of his 'friends' betrayed him, too. Especially those he was in an alliance with," I replied, hoping that my implications were clear with regards to my self-preservation.

"Why are you calling me, Kevin?" he asked softly.

"I'm calling you because you can get the word to the right people who might be interested in knowing he's been playing dead and more or less gone rogue. They may also wanna know he has Keyz in his custody, which means one of their own is about to be murdered. Aren't there rules against that sort of thing?"

"I'll take care of it," he replied, hanging up before I could say anything else.

"So what's the plan, son?" my mother asked again.

"The plan is to keep that sumabitch under attack until someone kills him. He can't have too many lives left, and it's beyond time for Satan to reclaim his soul. For now we're gonna continue to monitor the situation, and then we will be ready to knock his miserable head off when the time comes. Trust me, revenge is definitely ours."

Aryanna

Chapter 13

Devaughn Sr.

2027

The sound of my son's voice stopped the screaming in my head for a moment, just long enough for it to register in my mind what he was seeing right now. Before I could issue an order, JuJu was up the stairs to him and leading him away from a sight I was sure he'd never forget. The pain I felt in that moment was beyond any words that existed. No matter how right or wrong or how much destruction it had caused, I had loved Candy very much. And now she was gone.

"I told you to keep her safe, Blood," I said to 6'9" without looking up at him.

"Homie, I did my part, but didn't expect to walk into your house and it be some gunplay popping off."

I knew he was right, and just like Ramona, Candy's blood was now on my hands, too. But here wouldn't be the last of the blood spilled, not by a long shot. "Homie, I appreciate you coming all this way, but me and mine can handle it from here."

"Say no more, Damu," he replied, calling me Blood in Swahili. Slowly he backed out of the door, leaving us alone to grieve.

And we would grieve, but first we'd have our revenge.

"Get that bitch back downstairs, now! And if any of you motherfuckers let her so much as fart, I'ma end your life in a dramatic fashion," I told the remaining soldiers standing there.

I heard them get to work immediately, and then I felt Deshana come up beside me. She didn't say anything, but then again she didn't have to, because she knew just being there was enough. It said a lot that after all my years of gangbanging, I still felt the most protected and loved by my youngest daughter who was a Crip. That alone told me it was time to change the game and play it like a real chess master would. At this point the proof of just how misguided my loyalty had been all of those years was lying in my arms, so fuck what any oath had to say. It was time to trust my instincts and get back to the street mentality that had grown me.

Candy deserved a proper funeral and send off, but for now that would have to wait. I knew she would understand because she knew me better than most. Standing up with her still cradled in my arms, I carried her out the front door to my truck, where I laid her across the seat. I kissed her lips gently for the last time, closed the door to the truck, and closed myself off from every other emotion except the raw, unchecked rage coursing through my veins.

"Let's go," I told Deshana, walking through the door and taking the stairs back down to the room where Keyz was. When I walked through the door, I was greeted with the sight of Keyz strapped to the table and my mother strapped to a chair.

"Which one of you was guarding Keyz first?" I asked.

One of the soldiers raised his hand, and I calmly took the mac-11 from Deshana's hand. Without a word I released a flurry of bullets into his face and body, only stopping when his corpse stopped dancing and finally hit the ground.

"Let this be a lesson to the rest of you, because if you fuck up, you're dead. Period. Now, I want you to evacuate the house and take everything that is of value in a war. Empty out the panic room upstairs and any safes that are hidden. Make sure my son is out of the house immediately and guarded at all times."

"Dad, what are you doing?" Deshana asked.

"Making our next move, baby. Just trust me and make sure your brother is safe."

Her reply was to nod her head and kiss me on the cheek before following the others to the door. Before she walked out, she turned and asked me about her grandmother. I wasn't sure how I wanted to respond to that, but I could see the pleading for mercy in her bloodshot eyes. "She'll be fine," I told her before turning around to face my audience of two.

"Dee, you can't kill me. Think about our son," Keyz pleaded as I stepped to the table where I could look down on her.

"We don't have a son, bitch! You had a son! You sick, twisted slut. You had a son by tricking me, and now you think this life will somehow save yours?" I asked, feeling my body begin to shake from all of the anger bottled up.

"Devaughn, she has a point. Your son needs his mother, no matter how he was conceived," my mother said.

"My suggestion to you is that you keep your mouth shut. That's the only warning I'm giving you, understand?" I asked her softly, praying she would be smart enough to realize she could die as easily as anyone else at this point. Her silence told me she did.

The problem was even though I was beyond mad, I still understood just how unfair it would be to make an innocent little boy grow up an orphan. I couldn't be a father to him, not if I was being really honest with myself. I mean, how would that ever work when I'd constantly look at him and see his mother and all the pain she'd caused me? But he didn't ask to be born, either.

With my mind made up. I walked over to my mother and cut her restraints loose. "Listen to me very carefully, because I'm only gonna say this once. You're my mother, and I love you, but as of this moment you are now dead to me. I want you to take Keyz's son and leave Virginia tonight, and you're to never step foot in this state again. Since you're so concerned about him having a mother, you can be everything he needs. I'm giving you this chance because you're my mother, and despite our differences, I feel like I owe you that much. However, should you choose to disregard or disobey what I have said, then I will kill you and that bastard child without remorse or hesitation. Do you understand?"

"Son, I-I'm sorry, and I—"

"Do you understand?" I asked her again, not moved by her crocodile tears or her apologies.

She nodded her head yes before turning her teary, bloodshot eyes on Keyz one last time. I wasn't sure what she could be feeling for the traitorous bitch, nor did I care. Keyz had chosen her path, and now it was time to pay the piper.

"Take care of my baby, and give him all the love this world will never offer him. Pl-please, Ms. Gladys. Please tell him every day that his mommy loves him and will see him again one day."

"Oh, Kiara. Baby, I don't know why you did it this way, but I promise I'll take care of Devonte as if he were my own," my mother replied, wiping her tears away.

"Thank you! And just so you know, I did it for love. Even now I still love this man," she said, turning her bright eyes on me. I saw something of the girl I use to know in that moment, but it was too late for all that.

"Devaughn, pl—"

"Leave, Mom," I told her, letting her know my decision was final and not up for discussion.

"My lawyer will take care of everything, Ms. Gladys. Just take care of my baby."

"I will," she whispered, moving slowly toward the door and then out into the hall. "One day we all ask for mercy,

Devaughn. Remember that," she warned as her steps carried her out of my life forever.

Maybe she was right, but today wasn't my day to beg for mercy. Today vengeance was mine.

"Well, if I gotta go, I guess it's fitting that it be by your hand, huh, Dee? I mean after all, you did give me this way of life."

"Yeah, I did, but I don't know where this obsession you have came from."

"You don't? Really? Would you like for me to enlighten you?"

"If you want. I mean, these are your last moments, so you spend them how you want," I replied, inspecting the room for anything I didn't want destroyed.

"First off, I'm not obsessed with you. I love you. Some would say that's wrong, but I guarantee they don't really know you. They don't know how funny you are, or how sweet and thoughtful you can be. They don't know you're an excellent listener and you give profound advice. I mean shit, Dee, you came into my life when I needed you the most, when I was struggling to find myself and my place. Dad was my world, and when he died, I can't explain how lost I felt. I had nothing left except a mother who was a crackhead. You know how that goes, right?"

I just looked at her in response to her question, my face a blank mask void of emotion, because she didn't deserve my compassion or understanding. I owed her nothing at this point.

"You changed my world, Dee. You gave me the love and attention I needed when I needed it. You took me under your wing and made me feel special because you were teaching me the secrets of the world you lived in. For once I felt like I belonged. And with each letter we exchanged or conversation we had, I felt my love for you grow until one day I realized I was in love with you. Did you feel none of that?" she asked, her vulnerability plain to see in her eyes.

"What was I supposed to feel, Kiara? You're my fucking sister!" I told her, hoping somehow logical reasoning would make a dent at this point.

"We weren't raised like that, Dee! I saw you as a man, and I wanted you as a man. And you wanted me."

"What?"

"I know you felt something deeper. I know you thought about me the way I did you."

"Bitch, you're really loco, huh?" I asked, shaking my head with disbelief.

"Sir, the house is empty," one of the soldiers said from the doorway.

"Okay. Bring me a grenade from the stash taken out of the panic room, and bring a can of gasoline from the garage."

"Yes sir," he replied, leaving.

"Dee, I love you, and we can be together. Fuck what anyone has to say or what anyone thinks. We can rule the muthafuckin' world, my nigga, if you jus—"

"It ain't happening!" I yelled in her face. Her eyes flashed anger, but I could see the pain underneath. She really believed she loved me or was in love with me, but incest wasn't my thing. "All you've done is cause me pain, Kiara. Even if you weren't my sister, I could never love your devious ass. You don't deserve love. You deserve to be buried alive so you can have the knowledge death is certain and lonely. Luckily for you, I don't have the patience to kill you slow," I told her, flicking the razor from my mouth into my palm. For the first time I saw tears in her eyes, but I ignored it as I cut her pants and panties off.

"Wh-what are you doing?"

"Just stick around and you'll see," I replied, laughing. Just then the soldier came back and handed me what I asked for. In return, I instructed him to take the box with my baby's head in it upstairs to my truck.

Once he was gone again, I began dousing the room with the gas, not stopping until I'd soaked Kiara in it, too.

"Dee, please don't do this! I never meant to hurt you, I only wanted to love you," she insisted, crying hysterically now.

I ignored her pleas and concentrated on the task at hand. Unscrewing the top to the gas can, I stepped to the side of the table with the eight-inch tubing in my hand. Without warning, I shoved in inside her pussy until it was completely inside of her. My goal was to stretch her for what I had in mind, and I didn't care how much I hurt her in the process.

"Dee, don't!" she screamed.

There was nothing she could say to change my mind, though. Her life was over. I pulled the plastic tubing out of her and rammed it in again and again until I noticed her screams had taken on a different tone. I had succeeded in stretching her, but it was different, because her pussy wasn't resisting as much as it was sucking now. The sick bitch was actually turned on right now!

Let's see how long that lasted. I threw the tubing away, pulled the pin on the grenade, and proceeded to shove it inside of her. Now her screams were those of pain, and they were once again music to my ears. I felt her pussy tearing and felt her warm blood gush over my fingers before I finally had it inside her.

"Dee! Dee, pl-please! For da-dad!" she cried to me.

"For dad? You do know I never liked him either, right?" I asked, picking up the gas can, laughing.

Her response didn't matter, so I didn't wait for it. Leaving a trail of gas behind me, I made my way upstairs and outside until I was at my truck.

"She dead, dad?" Deshana asked.

"She will be," I replied, signaling for a light. I lit the trail of gas and watched as it raced back into the night with a whoosh.

"Let's go," I said, climbing into the truck next to the body of my sweet Candy Cane. Only Deshana rode with me.

By the time we got to the end of the driveway, the night sky behind us was alive and dancing with brilliant flames. Just as we turned the corner, I heard the first explosion, and it brought a smile to my face.

Chapter 14

2027

By the time we got to La-La's house and got set up, the sun was high in the sky and climbing. Looking out the window of her penthouse, I briefly saw how nice a day it would be before my mind closed in on the task at hand.

It was baffling to me how things had gone so wrong so fast. One minute I was awakened from the longest nap ever, and the next my whole fucking family was under siege. Five years had changed a lot, including the fear niggas had when it came to me and mine. That was about to change, though.

I could admit it was hard to focus with all the emotional turmoil going on inside me, but survival meant I had to find that hollow place within. As dangerous as I knew it would be to my psychological wellbeing, I had to let my mind be consumed by thoughts of murder. I needed complete focus on the task at hand.

Candy's body had already been taken to the funeral home, along with La-La's head. Neither I nor Deshana could deal with that right now, but it would get done.

I'd called to check on Ramona, and Sharday had given me hope by saying she was still alive. Still critical, but alive. I couldn't bring myself to tell her La-La was gone. I knew it would destroy her, because they were thicker than thieves. It wasn't just losing a sister, it was losing a best friend, too. I was use to loss and pain in my life, but I never wanted that type of ugliness to touch my children. It was time to make sure this shit never happened again.

Knowing everything that had happened, I thought Keyz's death would bring me more of a sense of peace, but the satisfaction was minimal compared to what I'd lost. Here I was at forty-three years old basically starting from the mud again, because I was just fighting for the survival of me and mine.

With Candy gone and Ramona on the verge, I had no idea what our holdings were. I didn't know friend from foe. I couldn't tell which smiles were hiding the deep-seeded hatred that wished death upon me. I felt like I was fighting blind, but I wasn't like most niggas who would run from that battle. I was just stupid enough to run toward it, because that's what my enemy wasn't expecting. I'd learned the importance of the art of unpredictability from the forty-eight laws of power, and in that moment I understand how it would save my life.

"La-La's partners are gathering all the records for your legitimate businesses, including the overseas accounts. Day-Day just called back and said Ramona's father is en route to the hospital. Apparently he heard about the shooting on the news," Deshana said, handing me a lit blunt.

"He and I need to sit down, so tell Day-Day to let us know when he arrives," I replied, hitting the sweet ganja and loving how it tingled my senses.

"Cool. Just to let you know, I sent all of your soldiers away, because I feel like me and my homies can give you more support at this point."

I gave her decision some careful consideration, liking the way it fit with my next move. The thing about corruption was you never knew how high up the ladder it went, so I don't know which Bloods to trust because I didn't know who Keyz had got to. "How many people you got?" I asked.

"We brought ten, but they've already been reaching out to the homies out here. Whatever you need, I gotchu, pop," she said, taking my hand.

My baby wasn't a baby no more. She was obviously a woman about her business. "Get your people to La-La's conference room for a meeting. I've got a few calls to make, and then I'll be there.

"Ok, Dad."

I hit the blunt again and passed it back to her before she went to rally the troops. Pulling my phone from my pocket, I dialed a number I hoped was still in service. It rang four times before I heard a familiar voice.

"Yeah?"

"Zone Six, Kirkwood," I replied.

He laughed at first, and I knew he was remembering the days when I'd shout that shit out across our pod. Me and him went back a dozen years or so, back to Bledsoe County Correctional Complex when we both were doing time in Tennessee. Our bond and understanding came from both being from out of town and being trapped inside the corruption that was the TDOC system. When we were locked up, the only way to make it and remain sane was to surround ourselves with real niggas. Real niggas were hard to find, though. There were so many suckers in the land of lollipops. Michael, A.K.A. Nutbutter, was a real nigga, and I needed that more than ever right now.

"What's good, Butter?"

"Shit, chillin'."

"My bad if I woke you up, bruh."

"Nah, you know I'm still on that penitentiary schedule, so I was up before the birds were."

"I hear you. Some habits can't be broken. Listen, I need you out here."

My request was met with silence, but I knew he was organizing his thoughts, because a call like this from me only meant one thing. "Send your info," he replied.

"It's on the way. And bring Happy Jack if you can locate him. I've got a job for him, too."

I heard his laughter all the way up until he hung up the phone.

Happy Jack was like an uncle to everyone in prison, and despite spending almost forty years behind the wall, he still had all his mental facilities. He kept a smile on his face and a hard dick for them "pretty" young white boys who came through the system, quick to show them the savage side of prison when he demanded they get their "funky ass out them drawls."

That was never my M.O., but I had a plan that required his special brand of justice.

My next call would prove the old saying of whether or not the enemy of my enemy was my friend or my enemy. The phone rang a few times, and then all I heard was silence and breathing. "It's DC, looking for Fish," I said.

There was some rustling on the other end, and then he came on. "What's up, DC?"

"I'm good, homie. Alive."

"I'd heard otherwise, so it's good to know that's not the case. What's good, though?"

"I need a face-to-face, and it's important."

"I dig that. I can be there by tonight if I push it, but I gotta tie up some loose ends."

"Take care of your business, but you ain't gotta worry about driving because I'ma send transportation. Can you be at Dayton Airport in about three hours?"

"Yeah, homie that straight."

"Ok, cool. And I need you to get with C-note too, a'ight. He's back in Nashville, but I'ma put the call in right now."

"We'll be there in a minute."

"I appreciate it, homie."

"It's nothing," he replied before disconnecting.

It wasn't always what you knew, but more so who you knew and whether or not you'd kept it real when it counted the most. A lot of muthafuckas rode with you when the times were good, but these days very few stayed when the chips were down.

Fish was actually J. Fishback from Knoxville, TN, one of the big homies for 43 Gangsta Crip and one of the smartest niggas I knew. C-note was the big homie for 107 Underground Crip out of Nashville, TN, and he was also a thinking man, which made us like-minded.

Before I'd ever become a blood, I was my own man, and that allowed me to see across the color divide and recognize the real in a muthafucka no matter what he repped. The calls I'd made were to men I knew I could trust, because this was life and death.

I sent Butter my info and told him who else would be coming from our old days locked up. With that important task out of the way, I made my way to my daughter's conference room.

When I opened the door, I noticed it wasn't that much different than my own, except the long conference table that dominated the room was a dark cherry wood. This was complimented by burgundy leather chairs and wall-to-wall burgundy carpet, along with a bar at the far end of the room that was made from cherry and marble. The walls were decorated with pictures of Sharday's album cover, as well as newspaper clippings from the high-profile cases La-La had won.

Despite my efforts to block it out, the ache in my chest intensified to the point it hurt to breath. My baby should've still been alive. She had so much life to live and so much to offer this world. It was still hard to believe she was gone, but I could never forget all she'd meant to me.

As I made my way to the seat in between Deshana and JuJu, I mentally assessed everyone in the room. There were seven guys and three females, not including Deshana and Ju. All three women rocked short hairdos, no makeup on the various shades of brown their faces came in, and somber expressions respectful of our loss, yet determined to avenge it. They had faces with no lines on them, speaking to their youth, but their eyes told stories of old souls who wished they could forget.

The men wore matching expressions. There were three on my side of the table. Two who were at least six feet and thick in the chest area with close-cut wavy hair. The third wore his hair in a high top fade and had a slender build. All of them shared the same coffee-colored complexion. The four men on the opposite side of the table were like steps in height, going from about 5'5" to 5'10". Two were obviously brothers because they had the same build, head shape, and intent look of distrust in their eyes. The other two were polar opposites: one light while the other was dark, and one fat while the other was skinny.

Overall, this didn't look like anything more than a group of college lads, but the best killers in the world didn't look the part.

"Before my father speaks, there's some things I need to say. I know for the last four or five years I've kept a lot of secrets with regards to my past, and that's mainly because it hurt too much to remember. I thought my father was dead. I thought he'd been murdered by a slob, and that played a big part in my decision to join this movement. You all became family, especially Ju, and none of that changes because my dad is now alive and well. I brought you all out here to settle his murder, and to make history by conquering what these east coast Bloods cherish the most: New York. I didn't expect us to step straight into a war, and I didn't expect to-to lose my big sister, or someone I considered family. But since this is the hand that's been dealt, I'ma play every single card in the deck, and reshuffle if necessary. The motivation remains the same, and for those of you that have lost someone you love, you should be able to understand why those I've lost have to be atoned for.

"Some of you look at my father and see an infamous Blood, but I promise you he's a man trying to come to terms with his losses and the betrayal of those he trusted the most. It'd be too much to ask you to put your life in his hands, but we've been through enough to ask you to put it in mine. If you can't, well there's the door, and there's no hard feelings. Make sure you stick with your decision, though, because this is a one-time offer," she concluded, looking around the room at everyone.

No one said anything, so she looked at me and nodded. I had a sense of déjà vu, but unlike the last time I addressed a room full of gang members, this wasn't about business. What I had to say was plain and simple. "We're gonna destroy any- and everyone who had a hand in this, and I promise if we do this my way, Bloods will cease to exist out here. Here's the plan."

Aryanna

Chapter 15

Devonte

2040

In the time it took us to get back to NY, I had learned quite a bit about my brother, more than probably even my father knew. To our dear old dad he might've been DJ the schoolboy, but to the underground world he was known as the whiz kid. Apparently he had inherited our father's business acumen, but he still wasn't ready for what the streets had to offer. It was gonna be my pleasure to teach his bitch-ass that lesson the hard way.

"It's Pinky," Ruby said, handing me the phone as we pulled up in front of my building.

"What you know, Pink?" I asked after sliding out of the truck and into my temporary wheelchair.

Pinky was a girl named Amber Lucille, one half of a dynamic duo that was a part of my team. Standing 5'0" and weighing 140 pounds with reddish-brown hair and a country twang, it was easy to be fooled by the sweet, innocent look she'd mastered. But deep down she was calculating and deadly, and that was why I loved her.

Her partner Joshua, or The Brain as we called him, was my money wizard. He had that non-descriptive, average white boy look that some might've called nerdish, but he had a mind for numbers like no one I'd ever seen or heard about. He was a gamer, so he spent his days in lands far removed from reality, and that somehow helped him get creative with both hiding and making money, not to mention stealing it when necessary.

"His operation and setup are pretty elaborate, but nothing The Brain couldn't understand and conquer. His base of operations seems to be Virginia for the moment since school has ended, but from what we can tell, his team is spread out across the country," she replied.

"Where is he now?"

"Our best guess is Virginia. The footage from the mall was useless because it was hacked and shut down. We don't even know where he entered or exited. His safest bet is to run home to daddy because he may have had money, and that can buy you protection, but without it he's a sitting duck."

"Had money? As in past tense?"

"Josh hit all of his bank accounts and drained them bitches a little while ago."

One thing I could say about my team was they knew how to fight, and they could do it without me holding their hands. "Good. Were you able to get a look at what my father has going on?"

"That wasn't as easy. From the look of things he's completely legit now, but his name is still feared from south central to Saigon."

I'd figured as much considering he'd been in the game for years and had managed to survive. As the elevator took us to the penthouse, one reality became crystal clear to me: Devaughn Mitchell's time was up. There was no way to go at his son, his namesake, while he was still alive. So he had to go.

"I ain't scared of him. We just need to bring him to us. Let me think on that for a minute, but in the meantime we need to get Brianna back."

I couldn't explain all I was feeling at the thought I might lose the love of my life. I couldn't live without her. I refused to!

"We're working on it, boss," she replied softly. "We're going after his second in command, some bitch named Harley Forts that's down in Virginia. We'll have her within the hour, and once we've got whatever info she has to offer, we'll use her to send a message."

"Keep me posted," I replied, disconnecting the call as Ruby rolled me into my apartment.

When I'd turned sixteen, my grandmother had moved one floor below the penthouse I'd grown up in, leaving it to me and Brianna. These walls held so many memories for me, going all the way back to the last day I'd been here with my mom. I felt those memories wash over me now in a flood of emotions, but I shut the lid on those tight and forced my mind to stay focused. "What time is our meeting?" I asked, wheeling myself toward my bedroom.

It seemed like forever since I'd been in this room we shared, but everywhere I looked I saw Brianna. Her red boy shorts were still where she'd dropped them on the black marble floor by the bed. Looking in the closet, I saw all the new lingerie she'd just bought for after our baby girl was born. Our closet floor was littered with all the new clothes and toys we'd gotten for our little one, and the bassinet next to our king size bed made my heart ache even more.

"Intelligence over emotion, my nigga," Ruby reminded me, walking past me into the closet.

I knew she was right. It was the first rule the big homies taught me. It was hard, though. I felt like a piece of my soul was missing.

"I'ma roll you a blunt while you take a bath," she said, laying some all-black billionaire jeans and a gray shirt on my bed. "The meeting is in twenty minutes, so wash your ass and let's get there."

My knee still hurt, but my Jacuzzi tub wasn't exactly wheelchair friendly. By the time I'd shuffled into the bathroom, ran my bath water, and gotten undressed, I was sweating like I'd just gone twelve rounds in a heavyweight fight.

"Here," Ruby said, passing me the blunt and then wrapped the waterproof knee wrap the doctor supplied me with around my knee before she stripped down and got into the tub with me.

"I want both of their heads, Ruby. It's long overdue."

"I know, my nigga, but we gotta go about this the smart way. It's obvious DJ is a hot head, and you know that's gonna be his undoing eventually. For now we play like a chess match, but you gotta trust the team around you. I'm my brother's keeper, feel me?"

"I do," I replied, passing her the blunt. We both washed the sex off of us, although from the look in her eyes it was hard not to let our guards down and get it poppin' again. We both understand there was no time for that, though.

"Do you still have my clothes here?" she asked, drying off.

"Yeah, in the spare room."

She went to retrieve them and I got dried off and got myself dressed. Twenty minutes after we'd arrived, we were back in my 2040 all-white Yukon Denali, hidden behind mirror tint and discussing strategy. Luckily the meeting place was only ten minutes away, and I had a valid reason to be late even though I was gonna get my ass chewed.

"You ready?" she asked on the elevator ride to the top of the Hyatt Regency Hotel.

"I guess," I replied, happy to be resting my knee by being back in my wheelchair.

Door number 7162 loomed in front of us when the elevator door opened. Ruby came from Blood royalty, and I guess I did too, in a way, but I knew I was in trouble for leaving NY without permission and putting my family in danger.

Ruby knocked, the door was opened, and we stepped into the lion's den.

"Peace, young Blood and Bloodette."

"Peace, almighty," we replied in unison.

"Come in and take a seat," Frank White said. Frank White was one of the oldest members of the council still alive, and it was an honor to sit down with him. The other two OGs present for this 93 council meeting were Mr. Flatline and Bloody Storm, the first female big homie to sit on the committee.

"Let's not waste each other's time," Frank White said. "Devonte, you fucked up and put yourself and your family in harm's way. That's unacceptable, and since Sunny Black is your direct superior, he will hand down your violation. Do you know what the five cardinal sins are?"

"I do," I replied hesitantly. I knew all too well I'd broken the rules when it came to breaches of security, and the consequences were severe.

"So you know what the punishment is?" Bloody Storm asked, looking at Ruby, who I'd felt tense up beside me the moment the first question was asked.

"I do," I said again, staring Frank White in the eyes without fear. One thing I'd learned about being a Blood is they rarely, if ever, gave a warning before they moved in for the kill. I was taught there was a certain precedent when it came to eliminating someone: one person to indicate the attack, one to clean up or finish the attack, and one person to keep an eye on anything else that could be perceived as a threat. A shooter, a catcher, and a safety. Me sitting here meant I was safe. For now.

"The reason you haven't been labeled and green lighted for termination is because we feel you're of use to the movement in a major way," Mr. Flatline said.

"For years you've had questions, and today you will get those answers. Your mother isn't missing, she's dead. I know you've probably always known this somewhere in your heart, but you probably held onto some hope like any good son would. You need to know the truth. I was the last big homie to see your mother alive," Frank White said. "We'd summoned her because she'd neglected her duties and her territories for five years. We assumed it was due to your birth, and that was somewhat understandable, but having you didn't mean she could stop being a Blood. What we didn't know at the time was who your father was or what your sister had done to him. However complicated their relationship, it wasn't our business, but we can't have warring within our own hood."

"Your father never quite understood that concept," Mr. Flatline interjected.

I was still trying to wrap my mind around the truth my mother was dead, she was really and truly gone. The pain was unspeakable.

"No, your father didn't understand that," Frank White continued. "He killed your mother and burned her house down. Of course a war ensued, but in the end Magod called a cease fire. No one knows why he did it or what your father could've possibly offered, but after this blatant attack on you, we're no longer inclined to keep the peace. You're one of ours."

"So what are you saying?" Ruby asked, speaking for the first time.

"We're saying," Bloody Storm replied, "that this is now a war. We're saying it's time Devaughn Mitchell died!"

Chapter 16

2040

I'd had a constant ringing in my head ever since we'd left the meeting with the council. All I kept thinking about and hearing was them asking me if I could kill my father. Could I? Did I really have what it took to take on the man, the myth, and the legend? There was no simple answer to that question, but only death would stop me from going at him.

"What's our next move?" Ruby asked.

At the moment me, her, the big homie Lamborgini Lyve for the Valentine movement, and the big homie Saint for the G-Shine movement were sitting in my living room putting our plans in motion. We had one thing in common when it came to my father: a need for revenge.

"Have we heard back from Pinky yet?" I asked.

"Not yet, but I'm expecting it soon," Ruby replied.

"Call her yourself, there's no time to wait. Lyve, Saint, my father has crossed the both of you and caused casualties within both of your hoods. With your help, I believe we can finally bring him to his knees."

"What do you have in mind, homie?" Lyve asked.

"We know DJ is my father's pride and joy, and now he somehow thinks he's a street nigga. Let's show the young boy what this life is like. If we attack both simultaneously, then one or both will fall. The pain of either will leave the other vulnerable. Because of the truce, my father won't expect all of our hoods to attack at once, and the element of surprise is our only advantage. Admittedly, he's expecting something because he can't be completely in the dark about his son's activities, but we're gonna move fast."

"How fast?" Saint asked with a smile of anticipated satisfaction creasing his face. It had been years since my father had carelessly slaughtered six G-Shine homies and crippled their hood by engaging in a war that wasn't sanctioned. But time didn't heal all wounds, and blood demanded blood in return.

"As soon as—"

"I got Pinky," Ruby said, interrupting me and handing me the phone.

"Talk to me. Pinky."

"We got her. She's outlined as much of DJ's business as she can, and she gave up the money he had hidden in exchange for her life," Pinky reported.

"There is no exchange. She doesn't get to live, understand?"

"I know. How do you want it done?"

There were several ways to die, and the way I was feeling had me thinking the more gruesome the death, the better. At the same time, this was about justice. "I don't care how you kill her, but I want you to put her body inside one of the legit businesses my father owns and burn it to the ground," I replied.

"Consider it done, where do you want us after that's taken care of?"

"I want you to sit up in a hotel in Virginia, because I'm on my way down. And I want The Brain to send me whatever information you were able to dig up on my father."

I heard her relaying my orders to Josh, and before I knew it my pone was buzzing from my incoming message. "You should have it. I'll call you back when we're in the hotel room and give you our location."

"Be careful," I warned before hanging up and addressing my captive audience. "To answer your question, Saint, that's how fast we're gonna move against them. Lyve, I know what went down between him and Murdaheart still has you feeling some type of way, so I'm sure you're up for a little payback."

"I never liked the idea of a truce with that nigga anyway, and I've been waiting to put his disloyal ass to rest," he said, smiling.

"Good," I replied, pulling up the information on my father to see how well it lined up with my next move. He probably assumed because he was legit that a muthafucka couldn't get at him, but I planned to show him just how wrong he was. "There will be casualties in this war, but they're necessary. My father thinks he can reinvent himself by becoming a legitimate businessman, but he fails to realize when you bring the streets to the business world, the business suffers. I want him to suffer."

"Lay it out for us, Tae," Ruby said, sitting next to me.

"I have a listing of his business holdings, and the plan is to burn those muthafuckas to the ground. With the support of your hoods, I believe we can hit a lot of them at once. And while he's dealing with the public fallout, we make our move against him in person.

"So you want us to burn them down tonight?" Saint asked.

"No, that's too easy. The casualties I mentioned earlier will be those of the people who work for my father. I don't care if it's a janitor or the CEO of the company, I want them dead."

"Doesn't he own boys' and girls' clubs?" Ruby asked.

"And? They ain't my kids. My kid is in his fucking son's clutches! This war is real! Now kill everything moving, because mercy is for the weak, and it ain't a luxury we can afford."

Aryanna

Chapter 17

Deshana

2027

The grounds of my father's plan was that it gave both immediate gratification as well as long-lasting effects. I'd always knew and respected his intelligence, but I'd never dreamed his mind had this many twists and turns. I didn't know he could be so patient, but I guess that was something he'd had to pick up in prison. I wished it was something he'd passed on to me, because I needed patience in a major way at this point.

The pain didn't lessen no matter how many hours or days passed. I still yearned to hear La-La's voice one more time. I felt so guilty for having missed so much in the last five years, and for cheating both of us out of all the memories we could've made. I couldn't verbalize how badly I wanted my big sister back, and with that pain came the tears that seemed to never end. I couldn't remember ever crying so much in all my life. I didn't know the body could produce this many tears!

"Hey, sis," JuJu said, coming into La-La's bedroom with a drink in her hand.

Since we'd all converged on La-La's penthouse, I'd taken her room as my own, needing to feel closer to her in any way. Most nights it was me, JuJu, and Sharday curled up in the queen size bed together, but somehow the room still felt empty. It was already sparsely decorated with just a dresser and two end tables accompanying the bed, not to mention the mirrors on the ceiling that told their own story. It was still so cold without her larger-than-life personality.

Sharday had taken the news harder than anyone once my dad had finally broken it to her. With her being by Ramona's side in the hospital, she had no idea what had happened to La-La, but once Ramona slipped into a coma, her father had her transported back to Italy, and Sharday stepped into this never-ending nightmare.

Complete and utter devastation was the only way to describe it. I'd questioned the wisdom in my father's decision to keep Day-Day here, but he insisted on having everyone under the same roof to better protect us. I didn't want protection, though. I wanted blood on my hands.

"Hey, Ju," I replied, sitting up and taking the drink from her. I swallowed the cognac in a single gulp, embracing its burn on the way down.

"I'm not gonna ask you how you feel because that's a stupid question. I just want you to know you're not alone in this, and I'll always be here for you."

I could only nod at her words because I knew she meant every one of them. In the two weeks that has passed, she hadn't left my side unless it was absolutely necessary, or if DJ wanted her. She'd been the only one who could get DJ to sleep, and whenever he woke up he cried if she wasn't within arm's reach of him. He wasn't her responsibility, but still she had stepped up like she always did.

Setting the glass on the nightstand, I pulled her into a hug and held her tightly.

"I know it hurts, but it'll get better," she whispered.

I don't know what came over me in that moment, but I needed to be closer to her. Pulling back from the hug, I looked deep into her eyes and saw the same love and loyalty I always had. Before I could question myself, I leaned forward and pressed my lips to hers gently. I felt her body tense immediately, but just as quickly it relaxed, and she opened her mouth to give me the kiss I really needed.

I'd never been with a woman before, although I knew Ju went that way sometimes, but in that moment it wasn't about what we were. I needed to feel loved completely, especially after Trey's betrayal. I needed to make lasting memories, because life was too short. Right then, I just needed!

"You sure?" Juju asked as our kisses took on a more urgent need.

I responded with actions by pulling off my white beater and shimmying out of my shorts, leaving me with nothing on. I felt the intensity of her stare as she took in every curve of my body, tracing it so thoroughly with just her eyes that I found myself thirsting for her touch.

When she dipped her head and took my nipple into her mouth I didn't know if I'd breathe again. She sucked it gently before biting it hard enough to send shock waves through my body. My hands went to her short hair as I pulled her closer, needing to feel her all over me. My pussy felt like Hurricane Katrina when her fingers gently parted me and dove deep inside, and she worked them like we were in the eye of a storm.

Just a touch so intimate from someone I loved and trusted made me cum instantly, and I felt my climax squirting all over her hand.

I was prepared to be disappointed when she pulled her fingers out of me, but watching her lick my trickling juices off of her hand had the storm rebuilding inside me at a frenzied pace. "Take your clothes off," I told her, getting off the bed and going into the master bathroom. I'd accidentally stumbled upon La-La's treasure chest when I'd first claimed her room, and right now I was glad I had. I selected a toy I wanted and went back into the bedroom, where I found JuJu naked, spread eagle and waiting.

It was like seeing her for the first time or with new eyes, but either way her body was amazing. Her skin was as flawless and appetizing as warm chocolate, and her body looked soft in all the right places. Her titties were modest, but I liked them that way, because I planned to put my hands around them and suck those blueberry gumdrops that were her nipples. She looked good enough to eat, and that's where I wanted to start.

Climbing up on the bed I laid the toy beside her. The look in her eye was challenging, but it also told me I'd have to take what I wanted, because she couldn't feel like she pressured me.

"Challenge accepted," I told her, putting her legs on my shoulders and diving into her sweet secrets. Starting with her clit, I licked and sucked her pussy until I felt the warm rush of her orgasm fill my mouth, but still I wanted more.

I grabbed the toy, which was a double-sided vibrating dildo, and slowly pushed one end inside of her throbbing, hot pussy. Pulling her into a sitting position, I angled myself just right and straddled my pussy on the other end. Looking deeply into her beautiful brown eyes, I set the pace to our lovemaking as I reached heights I didn't know existed.

"I-I love you, Ju!"

"I love you too, babe, always," she replied, taking my face in her hands.

She gave me the sweetest kiss I'd ever had, and then my world rocked as we came together. Still locked in our embrace, I felt my heart beating in sync with hers, and it made me smile. Once upon a time Candy had told me not to knock girl-on-girl action until I'd tried it, and damn was she right.

"You ok?" JuJu asked breathlessly.

"Uh. Uh-huh. You?"

"Never better, but where did that come from?"

"I-I just needed you," I replied truthfully.

Her response was to kiss me again, which caused my pussy to throb in rhythm with the toy still deep inside me. "Mm, save some for later," I told her, laughing.

"You promise?" she asked, pinching my nipples and causing me to moan involuntarily.

"Of course. There's no way this is a one-time thing."

"I'm glad you feel that way, because I've wanted you for a while now," she confessed.

I pulled back enough to disengage the toy so we could have this conversation with a clear head. "Why didn't you say anything?"

"Because, Deshana, I didn't wanna risk our friendship. I can't imagine my life without you right there with me, and I knew you didn't get down like that. At least I thought you didn't."

"You're my first and my last, Ju. I have no idea where this will go, but I know our bond is unbreakable. As for a relationship, I feel like we should have that conversation when death ain't around every corner, ok?"

"I understand. But if you die, I'd die, so let's make sure that doesn't happen, ok?"

"I gotchu, slim," I replied, kissing her again.

"Good, so let's get to work."

"What do you mean?"

"I just got off the phone with the fam out west, and they send their love. They also send info about who Trey is."

Aryanna

Chapter 18

Devaughn Sr.

2027

I'd been in wars before, and the price of victory had always been high, but I'd lost so much already that a part of me was scared to risk any more. I would never be scared of a fight or of any man who wanted to lock horns with me, but the pain? The pain I was feeling now was enough to swallow a city and drown it in mourning. I couldn't let it consume me, though. I had to use it as motivation in order to drown my enemies in their own blood.

The past two weeks had been some of the longest and hardest of my life, especially since I had to exercise extreme patience. I didn't wanna be patient. I wanted vengeance! The loss of my oldest daughter was still something I was fighting to comprehend, but I put on a brave face in front of everyone. And even though Ramona was still alive, I'd more or less lost her too. If not to a coma, then to time and space, because she was now out of the country. I understood her father's pain, and he understood mine, so I couldn't deny him his wish to bring her back to their homeland. There was a part of me that wanted her by my side as she had me by hers for the last five years, but I understood this war may never end. Not until I was dead.

Keyz may have been campaigning in hell for residency, but the fact of the matter was I'd killed a Blood without permission. Sometimes it was better to ask for forgiveness instead of permission, but I didn't want their fucking forgiveness. Too much had happened, and now all I wanted was their heads. They were only one way, one organization, but I had the support of Ramona's family as well as the Crip nation. All I needed now was to identify the muthafucka responsible for killing La-La.

Deshana told me all she could, which really didn't amount to shit considering how long they were in a relationship. I couldn't say that to her, though. She was already carrying enough guilt, and I wouldn't add to it. Truthfully, a weaker woman would've buckled under that type of guilt, but my baby was a warrior, and it was showing in this moment. For better or worse, she was like me. That's why I called her Lil' Me.

The sound of the balcony door opening behind me interrupting my thoughts, and I turned away from the beautiful view of DC at night to see who had joined me.

"It's hard to be afraid of heights with this view," Butter said, stepping to the rail and looking out at the twinkling lights.

"True, but I'm high anyway, so I'm not really worried about my fear of heights," I told him, laughing.

"You been high the whole time I've known you," he replied, laughing.

That was partly true, especially since we'd met at a time in my life when I was experimenting with all types of shit. "I think I had my midlife crisis at thirty. I mean, how else did you explain trying coke and meth that late in life?"

"I don't know, Roady. I use to wonder the same shit when you use to do that dumb shit. I think the time was just getting to you, but it could've been worse. Think about some of the niggas we were locked up with. There were some characters."

"You damn right!"

"Remember Big Boy?"

"Big Boy?"

"Yeah, you know Big Boy. Ronyet or something from Nashville that worked in the wood plant. Thirsty-ass nigga that was always lying about something."

"Oh yeah, whatever happened to him?"

"Dead. He gave that life sentence back, and when he got out them niggas he told on slumped him."

"Damn," I replied, shaking my head. I'd known the nigga was shaky, but I thought he was just a bitch-type dude. Everybody wasn't built to do time. "Whatever happened to Tiny?" I asked.

"Tiny who?"

"You know, Tiny from Chattanooga. I think his first name was Terrence or something. He had all that time for raping a bitch and beating her up."

"Oh! Him. Man, that nigga wasn't from Chattanoga. They don't build muthafuckas like him. And he was undercover."

"Undercover? Whatchu mean?"

"Nah, not the police, but he was speaking into the mic."

It took me a minute to catch what he was saying, but when I did I laughed until tears ran down my face. "Man, quit playing. Not dude. He was a holy roller, always going to church and speaking in tongues and shit," I said, lighting a blunt from the stash I had rolled on the table.

"He spoke in tongues, alright. Sucking dick and drinking cum. Not to mention getting fucked. Ask Happy Jack."

"Nah, homie, I believe you. I needed that laugh. It's been so long since I had a chance to genuinely laugh."

"I know, Roady. I won't pretend to know what you're feeling, but I'm here, and we're gonna handle it."

"I appreciate that, my nigga," I told him, handing him the blunt as the door opened again and Deshana stepped out with Juju in tow. "What's up, Lil' M?" I asked.

Even in the dim moonlight I could see the fire blazing in her eyes. "We know who he is. Everyone is in the conference room waiting on us," she said quickly.

This was exactly what I needed to hear, and I didn't try to hide the smile on my face as we made our way to the conference room.

We entered to find C-note and Fish smoking a blunt, huddled together and obviously going over strategy. C-note's six-foot, 200-pound frame was hunched over to accommodate the smaller Fish, listening intently to whatever he was saying. Fish may have only been 5'10" and all of 180 pounds, but he commanded respect wherever he went. C-note was the same way, but he had that light skin, pretty boy with dreads thing to contend with sometimes. He had to show muthafuckas he was serious. Fishback was a brown skin nigga with swag, but anyone could see the killer in him, even when he was smiling.

Happy Jack was posted up against the wall by the bar, dressed to the nines in a dark black billionaire suit with some blue and white Stacey Adams on his feet. A blue Dobb on his head with the peacock feather completed the ensemble. He looked like he stepped fresh out of the 1970s picture show, not a piece of lint anywhere or a wrinkle in sight. And he was a killer. The long, droopy face and quick smile might've convinced you otherwise, but I'd been in the belly of the beast with this broad-chest bastard, so I knew what he was capable of.

When you've factored in the stocky, quiet, no-nonsense killer that Butter was, I had a team capable of handling any task in front of us. I spoke to everyone and took my seat at the head of the table, waiting on my daughter to put her plan on the table.

"We just got word on who killed my sister and where he's from. When we dated, I knew him as Trey Wilson, but his real name is Kevin Treymane Holford. He came out west from Texas, but he's originally from Virginia, and he comes from money. His mom owns a trucking company that deals mostly with the import and export of things the law frowns on. Her name is Monica Holford. We didn't find much on his father other than he was some business man named T—"

"Timothy Williams," I said, finishing her sentence.

"Dad?" she asked, giving me a puzzled look.

"Do you remember Skino?" I asked her.

No one else in the room knew what we were speaking of, but Deshana had been in the room that night. She may not have seen him draw his last breath, but she knew who killed him. And now we both knew La-La's death was my fault. I hated myself for not seeing it sooner because no one outruns their past, and I had made a lifetime of enemies, which meant I should've known better.

"Dad, you couldn't have known," she said, almost as if she was reading my mind.

"Enlighten us," JuJu said.

"The night I was shot, I killed my big homie. To make a long story short, it was kill or be killed in the long run, so I did what I had to do. My big homie was Timothy Williams, and that means it's him and his family out for revenge."

My revelation was met with silence, everyone trapped in their own thoughts. I was glad my enemy finally had an identity, but the guilt I felt over La-La was suffocating me by the second. I didn't know how I expected to live with the knowledge I'd gotten my daughter killed. But before I got to that, I had some scores to settle.

"What's the play?" Fishback asked.

"Tomorrow we have my daughter's service, and then we hunt."

"Are you sure your plan is gonna work?" C-note asked.

"Ultimately, yes. In the meantime, the Crip nation will pick up more territory, which means more money. In exchange for your help, I will help with legalizing your money and building your own empire you can funnel it through. Agreed?"

"Agreed," Fishback said while C-note nodded his head.

"Big Jack, Butter, you will get $100,000,000 apiece so when all this is over, you can start over.

"Cool," Butter replied. "$100,000,000? And all I gotta do is burn a muthafucka's asshole up? Shit, then get the geese!" he said, laughing hard. His inability to say *grease* without his teeth in made us all laugh and lifted the mood. But only a little.

With everyone up to speed, I got up and headed back to the balcony. The beauty of the view was still there, yet my mind couldn't see it for what it was. I questioned how often my daughter had stood where I was standing, and I hated myself because she should still be standing here.

"It's not your fault, Dad," Deshana said, coming up behind me and taking my hand. Part of me felt like she was right, but I couldn't let myself off the hook that easy. "And your plan is a brilliant one," she continued.

My plan was simple, yet complicated. We were gonna kill as many Bloods as possible and take over their territory until the southern states were unified under a blue flag. Then we were gonna call a truce. Why? Because ultimately NY would burn, but that would take years of patience to achieve. If all went right, then one day a switch would be flipped and a nation's worst nightmare would come true. I was gonna make sure of it.

"Get some sleep, baby. I need you well rested for what comes next," I told her, kissing her on the forehead. She gave me a sad smile before going back inside and leaving me with my demons.

Sitting at the table, I lit a blunt and opened my mind to all the possible scenarios of how this thing ended.

The rising sun took me completely by surprise because I hadn't intended to sit there all night. I felt every year of my age when I stood up, but a hot bath would hopefully do the trick. I shuffled to the bathroom with my mind on autopilot, took a shower, and dressed in an all-black Gucci suit with matching loafers. Once I had my Glock .45 tucked into my holster, I was dressed, and I found everyone else ready when I came into the living room.

It was destined to be a hard day, but I gathered strength from having my selected friends and family there. La-La's mom would hopefully be well enough to show up. We loaded up into two black navigators and made the trip to the funeral home Keyz had bought awhile back. I didn't necessarily wanna do it there, but I needed a place that was discreet.

I still had no idea where my daughter's body was, so I used an empty, closed casket as representation. In my heart I knew a parent wasn't supposed to outline a child, so this all felt so wrong to me. We all just kinda sat and looked at the coffin, nobody wanting to offer up any hollow platitudes heard at so many funerals. The pain of our loss was beyond words.

"I come to pay my respect, big homie," he said, walking into the funeral home with five homies in tow.

I hadn't heard his voice in years, but my instincts still reacted with the same mistrust as always. "What's poppin', Murdaheart? It's been a long time."

Aryanna

Chapter 19

DJ

2040

There was no real way to prepare for a war if I'd never been through one before. Physically I could be ready and strapped like the army, but the mental fortitude only came from survival. I thought I knew everything there was to know about war, but the savages that had raised Devonte had given him a different education. He was as ruthless as our father, if not more so, and I knew I had to hit that learning curve quickly or die.

I turned the TV off when she entered the living room carrying the baby, not wanting her to see anything that would shift her focus from that bundle of joy. The first month had been hard on all of us, especially with the baby being premature. Brianna was on edge constantly, barely eating or sleeping because she was always hovering over her daughter. I was worried too, but I was also on edge about the war I'd started.

I'd thought my father had been exaggerating when he said shit had gotten real, but I was wrong. $300,000,000 had vanished into thin air, plus the $120,000,000 that I had stashed, and not even The Mad Hacker could figure out where it was. Since my stash was discovered, it was a safe bet Harley had told everything she knew before she died, forcing me to shut down my entire operation. My money and power had disappeared overnight, not to mention my father was under attack, too. Twelve of his businesses were burned to the ground, over fifty people were killed and another seventy injured, including twenty kids. These muthafuckas were merciless!

I was man enough to admit I was in over my head, but bitch wasn't in my blood. If they wanted a war, they would damn sure get one. If my pops ever made up his mind on our next move.

"Give her to me," I told the visibly exhausted Brianna. She didn't like me or trust me, but I'd been nothing but a gracious host during her imprisonment in my home. Plus I could get the baby to sleep.

She handed her to me, and immediately her crying quieted as I rocked her back and forth. "I don't understand how you do that shit," she said, disgusted.

My laughter didn't help. It only earned me a hard look. Her face was easy to look at, though, and her body had snapped back with a vengeance. Must've been the breast-feeding.

"Don't hate, slim. I'll teach you my secret one day."

"Whatever. You two just have a bond I don't understand, and her and I just feel so disconnected."

"Well, maybe if you stopped referring to her as 'her' and gave the baby a name, it might help." My suggestion was met with silence, but I could read the contemplation in her eyes.

"I did have a name in mind, but I don't know."

"Tell me. It can't be as bad as some of the ghetto-ass names black folks come up with."

"Hope. What do you think of naming her Hope?"

"That's. Actually, that's perfect, considering all we went through bringing her into the world."

"I thought so, too. I was thinking, though."

"What were you thinking?"

"Despite the circumstances, I feel like I owe you for saving her life. And since I now know you're her uncle, I think it's ok if you give her a middle name."

I didn't expect this request in the slightest, not even with everything that had happened. "You're crazy," I told her, trying to laugh it off.

"I'm serious," she replied, looking at me intently.

Looking down at the sleeping baby in my arms, I felt something I couldn't quite explain, but I knew it meant I'd protect her before ever hurting her. "Anything I want?" I asked.

"Within reason, fool."

"How about Amazing? Hmm, Amazing?" I said, kissing her tiny head.

"We need to talk though, DJ."

"About?"

"The obvious."

"Hold on. Intercom on. Page CJ to the living room."

Kristi stayed on in the main house to make sure little Hope was okay, but I'd hired a private nurse to live in my house and be on call 24/7. Her name was Casey Jean, but we called her CJ, and she was great with children. Not to mention beautiful.

As soon as the intercom went off, she appeared like magic. She stood maybe 5'4" with long black hair, and she had those bedroom eyes a man could get lost in. Cute in the face and thick in the waist was how I liked them, and she was definitely that.

"Can you put her in her nursery?" I asked, handing Hope to her.

"Sure," she replied, giving me her sexy smile and winking at me.

"Okay, Bri, you have my attention," I said, sitting in the leather chair across from her on the couch.

"You've had me captive for a month. You shot my fiancé in front of me. Yet this doesn't seem to be who you are for real. It's almost like you're wearing somebody else, and I wanna know why. I've never heard of you, never heard Devonte speak about you, and then out of nowhere you show up like the fucking Grim Reaper! Why?"

"It's complicated."

"Then uncomplicated it for me. I mean, obviously your father has a lot to do with it because he knows me and I've never heard of him either. Just break it down for me."

Where did I begin, and did I even owe her and explanation? It wasn't like she could understand the horror of it all anyway, so what was really the point? "You wouldn't understand."

"Try me. Don't you think you owe me that much?"

"What do you know about his mother and our father?" I asked hesitantly.

"Nothing. I've known Tae since middle school, and we don't have secrets, but his mother has always been an off limits topic of discussion."

What she said made sense considering how ugly the truth could be, so maybe it was time to turn the lights on all the skeletons in the closet. "Devonte's mother more or less raped our father."

"Don't feed me bullshit, DJ. Women don't rape men because men stick their dicks in anything. Be honest or just say you don't wanna talk about the shit."

"I was honest, and if you'll shut up, I explain it all."

She said nothing and gave me the go ahead gesture to finish the story. I laid it all out for her as quickly as I could, hating the taste the truth left in my mouth. The slack-jaw look she gave at the story's conclusion told me she couldn't believe it, but she believed me.

"So that's why you want him dead? But I still don't get that part," she said.

"One night when I was five, his mom attacked us here at the main house. She came with her goons and tried to kill everyone here, but at the time she didn't know my father was alive. In a coma, but alive. I witnessed that gunfight, and later that night I saw his mother kill my mother. It took me awhile to understand and comprehend what had happened, and my father tried to keep me in the dark. No secret lasts forever, though. I wanted him dead because his mother killed mine. I wanted him dead because he should've never been born. But now I want him dead because he's as twisted as his mother is, and he has no regard for human life."

"What do you mean?" she asked, puzzled.

I hesitated at this question. How much honesty did I really owe her, and how much did I want to give? At this point it wasn't completely about her, though. I'd helped bring her daughter into the world, and in some ways that made me responsible for her life. What would her life be like if Devonte raised her?

"TV on," I said, looking at her.

"DJ, talk to—"

"Your answer's on the screen."

She shifted her focus from me to the TV, and I watched her expression go from annoyance to complete horror. The news was broadcasting the latest attack, which was on a boys' and girls' club in Petersburg, VA. They were showing the bodies being carried out as well as the bodies littering the street where they'd tried to escape the fire only to be gunned down. Most of the bodies were under four feet tall.

"What? What is that?" she whispered. I'd kept her in the dark, allowing her only to watch movies since she was captured, but now the truth was out.

"That's a boys' and girls' club owned by my father. That's Devonte retaliating against us. That's what he's capable of," I told her dispassionately.

I heard her dry heave before she bolted toward the bathroom. "TV off," I commanded, getting up and walking to my office.

I sat down at my desk intending to face-time with The Mad Hacker, but before I could begin I was interrupted by a knock on the door.

"What's up, CJ?"

"She's sound asleep. Anything else you need?"

"Nah, I'm…" I hadn't noticed the look in her eyes until just then. It had been a long month without Coco. My father locking down both houses made it impossible to see her. "What did you have in mind?" I asked her.

She stepped into the room and pushed the door up a little behind her. Still looking at me as she bit her bottom lip, she stripped off her scrubs until all she had on was a pink and white panty set.

"Take that off, too," I told her, sliding back in my chair and pulling my dick out.

She did as she was told, and then came around the desk to me. I saw her eyes widen a little at the size of me, but the licking of her lips told me she was up for the challenge. "May I?" she asked seductively.

"Mmhmm."

She took me in her mouth until my dick was knocking at her tonsils like a DEA raid. I'd never had my dick sucked so thoroughly. I mean, she was licking my balls and everything. I felt my toes curling until I felt the heat of her stare. I didn't know how long Brianna had been standing in the door, but there she was, looking on intently.

"Come here," I told CJ, pulling her head from my lap and sitting her on my dick without her knowing we had company.

"Oh, shit!" she moaned, struggling to take all of me inside her at once. Her pussy was so tight and hot, not to mention ridiculously wet.

Grabbing a handful of her hair, I locked eyes with Brianna as I pushed up inside of CJ, loving how her tight pussy sucked me in and didn't wanna let go. I expected Brianna to turn away, but instead she crossed her arms and leaned against the door jam, eyes taking in the show.

"Harder!" CJ demanded, and I complied with her request.

The only thing I was asking myself was who exactly was I fucking? Was it CJ or Brianna?

Aryanna

Chapter 20

Devaughn Sr.

2040

"What are you gonna do?"

"You know what I'ma do, Kristi."

"I know what you feel like you have to do, but Devaughn, you've worked so hard not to be that man anymore. You changed."

"I have changed, but some things will never change, and I can't just roll over and die."

"I'm not suggesting that," she replied patiently. "But you're his father, whether you like it or not, and right now he needs you. He's screaming for help!"

This statement caused me to look at her closely, trying to see whether or not she was telling a bad joke. Her expression was earnest, though. It must be the blond hair or something, because normally she gave sound advice and insights, but this was crazy. "My help? Kristi, they've destroyed twelve of my businesses, and their latest exploits include slaughtering children. Yeah, he does need my help. To die."

"Devaughn, you can't kill him. He's your son!"

"Correction, he's Keyz's son."

The comment earned me a look of annoyance from her blue-green eyes. I'd been on the receiving end of that look for many years now, so it didn't faze me, and she knew it. "Devaughn," she said quietly. That tone of voice did faze me, though, and she knew that as well.

Our relationship was one full of complications. I mean, technically she was my stepmother at one point, but she'd become my best friend during my time behind the wall. The love I had for her surpassed all understanding. If I was honest with myself, I could admit my relationship with her was one of the realest I'd ever had until Belinda had come along. As twisted as it seemed, me and Kristi had been in love once and had even talked about marriage. Maybe I had been rebounding and still reeling from losing Ramona to a coma, but either way we had taken our relationship to the next level.

And then I met Belinda Diane, a 5'7", hazel-eyed stallion who was so much more than beauty. She had swag, she had the knowledge of the streets, and she had heart. All of those things captured my heart, and just like that the relationship between me and Kristi had run its course.

The aftermath of that storm had been rough to weather because I loved and respected Kristi, and so I fought for our friendship. It was worth saving. The only problem was we hadn't stayed just friends.

"What do you want from me, woman?" I asked, exasperated.

"I want you to be the man I know you are deep down, and stop giving in to your baser instincts," she replied, snuggling closer to me in the bed.

"That's funny, considering me giving into my baser instincts is what got you in my bed right now," I said, holding her close. Her response was to bite my nipple lightly and let her tongue dance with the hair on my chest. "Don't start," I warned.

"Will you at least consider having a sit-down with Devonte?" she asked, rolling on top of me and aligning herself perfectly for penetration.

"Are you seriously trying to negotiate from that position?" I asked, slipping my dick inside of her.

She didn't say a word, just began the slow gallop we both loved so much. In my younger years I had been something like a pimp, or maybe a whore depending on who you asked. But since Belinda I had only fucked one other woman, and she was astride me at the moment, pinning me to the bed with her tight, throbbing, wet pussy. At 5'1" and 160 pounds she was tiny, yet thick enough to take a punishing in the bedroom. And she was a freak!

"I'm in the perfect position to negotiate, sweetheart, and do you know why?" she asked seductively.

"Mm. Why, baby?"

"Because I'm on top," she replied, hopping up before I could grab ahold of her, laughing like shit was funny.

"Not cool! Come on and quit playing," I told her, still lying on my back with my manhood pointed at the sky.

"Give me what I want and you can get what you want."

"I will not be blackmailed into this."

"No, but you will be whitemailed into it if you want some more of this good shit. So, do we have a deal?"

"Yes, do you have a deal, Devaughn?" Belinda asked as she came through the bedroom door.

My tongue was stuck to the roof of my mouth, and I couldn't utter a word, let alone formulate a sentence. This was bad. All bad. "Uh! Baby, what are you doing back? I told you to stay where it was safe," I managed to mumble weakly.

"I saw the news and I didn't want you going at this alone. It seems you ain't alone though, you sorry muthafucka!" she spat, looking directly at a visibly shaken Kristi.

Kristi may have been a lot of things, but a gangsta she was not. Thankfully she was smart enough to keep her mouth shut.

"Baby, this ain't nothing, I swear."

"Just like you swore it was friendship between you and this trifling bitch? How convincing do you think that is at this moment?"

I didn't have an answer for that, and I could only hurt myself by kicking bullshit at her. Kristi was a white girl, but Belinda was a white girl from the projects, which meant she was not for the shit. This was gonna end bad.

"I'm sorry, babe. That's all I can say at this point."

"I told you I would leave you if you ever cheated on me, Devaughn, but I never liked this bitch anyway, so there's no way I'm letting her win," she replied, pulling her pearl-handled 9mm from her purse.

I'd given her that gun as a birthday present, and right about now I was regretting it. I hopped out of the bed, feeling a sense of déjà vu as I stood between two women I loved.

"I suggest you move. You know I ain't playing," Belinda said, flicking the safety off her gun.

"This ain't her fault. I'm the one you're really mad at, so deal with me."

"You know I'm not gonna fucking shoot you, boy. But I never liked this bitch, and it is her fault because she's taking dick that don't belong to her. She couldn't keep her legs closed, so the whore gotta pay for that."

"Baby."

"Look, Devaughn, you need to focus on what's really important, because there are people trying to destroy you, and you have yet to retaliate. Pussy is what started all of this shit, and look at what you're doing now. Is this ho worth your family? While you're so concerned with getting your dick wet, have you even once thought about what all this means for your other kids?" she asked with tears swimming in her beautiful eyes.

Her words cut worse than a razor could, because I knew she was right. This was a war that involved both of my sons, but I still had my daughters to worry about as well. After all the mistakes I had made with La-La, Sharday, and Deshana, I would think I had learned the cost of not putting family first. It had to be family over everything or it didn't mean shit at all in the end.

"Nothing is worth my family, and I will do everything I can to protect them."

"We can talk about that after we handle this situation, don't you think?" She said, letting me know she wouldn't be distracted that easily into forgetting what she'd walked in on.

"Baby, please!"

"Begging ain't gonna turn this into a threesome, now move the fuck out of my way!"

She was pissed, and I knew this because it was rare she came at me sideways. I loved her, though, and I knew I was wrong to hurt her, but how could I let her kill Kristi? "Give me the gun."

"Devaughn, how are you just gonna let her put her hands on me?" Kristi asked, bewildered.

We'd been through a lot together, so at the very least I owed her an explanation. "I've been in this position before, and I didn't make the right decision. I can't go through that again," I told her.

"That's absolute bullshit! After all the shit we've been through, this is how you do me? You're a piece of shit, just like your father was."

Her words shocked me. I mean, she had never just flown off the handle like that. Who did she think she was talking to?

"I'ma let that go because I know you're upset, but don't talk to me like you don't know who I am," I warned.

"Oh, I know just who you are, but do you know?"

"What the fuck is that supposed to mean?"

"Wouldn't you like to know, you bastard?" she said with a malicious smile on her face.

Smiles tend to hide a lot of thoughts, but I still saw the very real fear in her eyes. "Last warning," I told her seriously.

"Fuck you! I should've never got involved with you anyway, especially after all the shit you've put me through. That's okay, though, because now I really know you don't give a fuck about me, and I don't give two fucks about you."

"Really? Ok then," I said, taking the pistol from my wife's hand and stepping out of her way. "Get her!" I ordered, laughing at the disbelief on Kristi's face.

The first punch was followed by a wet crunching sound, which usually signaled a broken nose, but not in this case. Belinda's punch had landed squarely in Kristi's right eye, shattering her eye socket and leaving her grabbing her face, screaming. It was evident my wife still had that B-more street life in her West Virginia upbringing. She fired punches in a furry, first causing Kristi to double over, then standing her straight up with an uppercut to the chin.

"Baby, you're getting blood on the floor," I told her, moving out of her way as she continued to work.

"Shut up!" she grunted, swinging a right hook that turned Kristi's world upside down when she landed on her face.

When she started kicking her, I turned my back and started getting dressed. I felt bad. This was my fault and shit was getting out of control fast.

"Enough," I said once I was dressed.

"Stay out of this!" Belinda yelled, bringing her foot down on Kristi's ribs.

"I said enough!" I picked her up and carried her across the room, away from the bleeding and whimpering woman on the floor. "Intercom on. Page Deshana to the master suite. Emergency!"

A sound like a tornado warning came over the speakers in my house before the message was broadcast, and moments later Deshana came running through the bedroom door. "Dad?"

"I'm good. Help me with this mess."

"What the fuck? What's going on?"

"Your daddy can't keep his dick in his pants," Belinda said, still struggling in my arms.

"What else is new? Damn, did she do this to Kristi?"

"Just get her up and out of here, please!

"I hate you!" Kristi yelled, sobbing and trying to hold her eye in her head.

"The feeling is mutual, bitch!" Belinda shouted back.

I watched as my daughter peeled Kristi off my white carpet floor, still admiring her naked body, until her comments registered in my mind. "What did you say?" I asked her, sitting my wife down and moving toward her.

"I said-I said I hope he kills you! I only wish I'd done it first, like I did him."

To others this comment made no sense, but I knew exactly what she meant. Years ago my family had suspected Kristi had actually killed my father after one too many ass-whoopings. The problem was she was a nurse, and it had looked like he dies of natural causes, so proving foul play was almost impossible. All we had were suspicions, until now.

"You. You killed my father?" I asked, taking a step toward her.

Her response shocked me, because she actually had the nerve to start laughing in my face. "No, you dumb fuck, I killed his best friend."

"I don't understand," I replied.

"Do you really think I would've fucked my own stepson? Or planned a future with you all these years? News flash: I wouldn't have, and I didn't. Your father wasn't your father, but your whore of a mother never told you how she was fucking him and his partner."

Her words hit me with the force of a machine gun round, threatening to take me off my feet. At my age, daddy revelations shouldn't have rocked my world like this, but I was truly standing there speechless. What she'd just revealed turned everything I knew completely upside down, if it were true. "You're lying, bitch," I replied weakly.

"Am I, Devaughn? Ask your mother, then. Ask her after you kill your own son," she said as Deshana dragged her from the room.

And that's when the weight of the world hit me between the eyes. If my father wasn't my father, then Keyz wasn't my real sister.

And Devonte was as much my son as DJ was.

Chapter 21

Devaughn Sr.

2027

Murdaheart still looked the same, as if time had stood still on him for five years. I couldn't quite pinpoint where my mistrust had come from, but I attributed it to there just being too many questions surrounding his loyalties. We hadn't had a face-to-face meeting since the one at my house, and while his soldiers had leant some support during the war, after that I still hadn't felt the presence of the Valentine homies like I thought I would.

My initial reaction was to ask him what it was exactly he wanted now, but my analytical mind took a leap to another conclusion before I could open my mouth. There were two more pressing questions: how did he know I was here, and how did he know I was alive?

"You came to pay your respects?" I asked, standing up to face him.

"I did, homie. I'm sorry for your loss," he replied extending his hand to me.

I took it and pulled him into an embrace, my eyes briefly locking with Deshana's, making my message clear. "I appreciate the sentiment, but how is it you know anything at all about me and mine?" I whispered in his ear.

I felt him jump and wanna reach for his gun when Deshana and JuJu made lunch meat of his entourage with their harmonious duet of pistol play, but I held him tight. "Do you think I'm stupid, nigga? No one knows I'm alive or that my daughter was murdered, yet you show up?"

"I can explain, homie, please. Just listen for a minute."

"Oh, I'm dying to hear your explanation, because I'm sure it'll prove entertaining at the least. But for your sake, it better be of some use to me. Deshana, you, C-note, and Fish put them bodies in the back. Butter, post up at the door. JuJu, get a chair to strap this nigga to. And Happy Jack, get ready to work."

Everybody moved without question. I took the .44 Murdaheart had been trying to reach for and tucked it into the back of my pants before handing him over to JuJu. Once he was secured to the chair, I dragged him right next to my daughter's coffin, wanting to further impress upon him how real this moment was.

"Start talking," I commanded.

"I know who is really after you besides your sister."

"Really? And how did you come upon this information?"

"I, uh. I had some business dealings with him because he's part owner in a trucking company. I didn't know who he was at first, so—"

"And when did you find out who he was?"

"It wasn't until he contracted me to kidnap the Vicks family."

"You kidnapped my nigga Vick's wife and kids?"

"It was business, homie, and—"

I interrupted his sentence by slamming the butt of his pistol across his eye, splitting it on contact and letting blood run freely. Vick's family meant there was more blood on my hands, because he wouldn't have been involved if it wasn't for me.

"Homie, listen!" Murdaheart pleaded, blinking his almost-closed and bleeding right eye.

"Talk, nigga."

"I didn't know why he wanted them snatched because I didn't know about your friendship or your business relationship. I didn't suspect shit until he called to tell me you were alive still."

"And why the fuck he called you?"

"Because he's scared of you! That phone call made me and my team dig deeper, and that's when I found out he was Skino's kid. Everything made sense. Now I'm here to fill you in."

"Really? And how did you know my daughter was dead?"

"You haven't seen the news in the last 24 hours?"

His question caused an unease to creep around my heart, because there was no way this could be good. "No, I haven't. Why?"

"Because a headless body was fingerprinted, and the match was immediate given, the well-known lawyer she was. The cops have a lot of questions, considering all the activity at that location and then torching the main house. I thought you knew all this, fam."

I hadn't known any of it, and hearing it all from his mouth was even more unsettling. Skino's son was obviously smarter than I'd given him credit for, because attracting attention from cops and the news meant I couldn't just walk around like I was legal. No one knew Candy was dead, and with Ramona being out of the country, that meant the cops would have more questions than answers. That was like giving a dog a brand new bone. Still, I didn't trust this nigga in front of me. The best lies were ones that incorporated a lot of truth, plus I knew this muthafucka's loyalties could be purchased, which meant he wasn't loyal at all. He'd do perfectly to send my message, though.

"What else can you tell me, homie?" I asked patiently.

"Just that he's trying to get the nation to do his dirty work and come after you, and he's gonna continue to make moves against you."

"Moves? Like what?"

"Going after your family."

"I've got them all guarded now."

"Do you? Including your babymama?"

"I—" It struck just then how odd it was Mikko wasn't there yet. She was supposed to have gotten a day pass away from St. Elizabeth's to say goodbye to her daughter, but she wasn't there. "JuJu, find Deshana and find out where her mom is. Be safe," I warned as she disappeared down the same hallway my daughter had minutes ago. I turned my attention back to the blubbering man in front of me, once again forcing myself to lock away my feelings of fear. Mikko would be alright. I was gonna see to that.

"So you came to me with this info because?"

"Because we're homies, Blood. I am you and you are me, that's the oath we took."

"That is the oath we took, but somewhere along the way most of you bitch-niggas forgot what that meant. Somehow you put an 'I' in the word 'team.' You muthafuckas ain't loyal to nobody but your goddamn self! And that's okay. And since the definition of real ain't universal, I'ma show you what real is, my dude. Happy Jack, you ready?"

"Get him out of 'em," he replied, taking his suit jacket off and folding it across a chair.

I stepped up to Murdaheart and smacked him across his head with the pistol, just hard enough to daze him a little. Flicking the razor out of my mouth, I cut his restraints loose and then rebound his hands and feet together so he couldn't fight back or run. I cut a clean slit down the back of his pants, and then tore his pants and underwear completely off.

"Where you want him, Jack?" I asked.

"Put him back in the chair with his juicy ass facing me," he said.

I did like he told me, and then pulled the phone from my pocket to record what happened next.

"What? What the fuck are you doing?" Murderheart asked, slurring his words heavily, but conscious enough to know his bare naked ass was blowing in the wind.

"Well, to put it simply, homie: if it's fuck me, then it has to be fuck you. Loyalty ain't something you can buy, because real niggas do real things. You should've learned that long ago."

"Devaughn, you can't be serious! Homie, I was just—"

"Shut up all that damn noise, now. You lucky I'm using grease on your funky ass," Happy Jack said, stepping up behind the squirming Murdaheart and dropping his pants.

"Whenever you're ready," I told Happy Jack, hitting the record button on my phone and pointing it at Murdaheart's face.

The first screams were a thing of beauty as Happy Jack not-so-gently shoved his dick inside him. In prison, rape is as real for men as it is for women, and since I'd known Murdaheart on the inside, I knew this was a worst nightmare come true. For Happy Jack, it was another day at the office, and from the pounding he was giving Murdaheart, I could tell he enjoyed his work. For me it was a sample platter of revenge.

"Oh nah, nigga, if you thought shitting on this dick would stop it from cumming, you got me fucked up," Happy Jack told him, grunting harder and pumping faster.

I kept on recording, moving around to make sure all of his humiliation was captured. His screams brought C-note and Fish from out of the back, but they pulled up short once they saw how it was going down. By the time it was over, he'd screamed so much he lost his voice, making his protests sound like those of a mentally retarded person. I couldn't hold my laughter in.

Once Happy Jack had gotten off, I turned the phone toward me to issue my statement. "All of you are fucked," I said, then I stopped recording.

"Now what?" Fish asked.

"Now we get it on without remorse. God made it rain for forty day and forty nights. Let's see if we can break that record, substituting rain drops for bodies. You with that?" I asked him.

"You know I am," he replied.

"Well, consider this my first gift to you. This is Murdaheart, a big homie for the Valentine Blood movement. He just told me he kidnapped my nigga Vick's family, and you know how the game goes, so that means they're dead. Vick is a 43 gangsta under Cartoon out of St. Louis, and he controls part of Virginia. More than that, though. Vick was my dude, and he didn't deserve that shit, so I'm giving this muthafucka to you, and you can kill him how you want."

"That's what's up," he said, shaking his head.

"Butta?"

"Yeah, Dee?"

"You ready for this?"

"Ain't nothing left to talk about."

"Dad!" Deshana yelled, coming up behind me.

"What is it, baby?"

"He's got Mom. She hasn't been there, and they don't know exactly when she went missing."

I could see the panic all over my daughter's face, stealing her youth in that moment and making her almost unrecognizable. I couldn't let her continue to be hurt like that, to lose everything and everyone that mattered to her. It was time to play offense instead of defense.

"We'll get her back, sweetheart. I promise."

"How can you promise me that, Dad? After all that's happened?"

"Because no one gets away with fucking with my family. No one."

Aryanna

Chapter 22

Devonte

2040

"Oh!"

"I'm cumming, too!" Ruby yelled, arching her back and throwing her pussy at me harder. Her and I had one bed while Pinky and The Brain had the other. Pinky was riding her man while looking at me, and I was blowing Ruby's back out watching her, the sexual tension so thick it felt like we were touching across the room.

I watched closely as Josh pulled her hair and she rose higher until I saw her titties dancing to a beat of their own. The flush of her skin and the hardness of her nipples turned me on even more, and I used that motivation as I dug deeper inside Ruby's pulsating pussy. I felt her cum drench my dick before she collapsed face-first on the bed, exhausted from our workout.

It was 2:00 a.m., and we'd all been fucking and sucking since 8:00 p.m. the previous night. It was truly amazing what the combination of ecstasy pills and Viagra could do, especially after Ruby started poppin' shit about how she could take dick. The girl had heart, but she continuously ended up tapping out in surrender.

I knew we were in for a long stay down here, which was why I suggested the double bed hotel room, so we could entertain each other. Each couple had pushed the other to different heights of freaky shit, celebrating every day of victory against my father and brother.

But after a month, I was of a mind to up the ante just a little, and the look in Pinky's eyes said she was down to do the same. The Brain would do whatever she wanted because he was pussy-whipped, but Ruby was the wild card in the bunch. I wasn't in the mood for no drama. Life was good at the moment, considering the mighty Devaughn Mitchell wasn't even fighting back.

They came in a noisy celebration, and The Brain collapsed on his back, sucking in some much-needed oxygen. Pinky climbed off him and walked into the bathroom, giving me an eyeful of her juicy ass and pussy, making my mouth water a little. When she got to the bathroom door, she paused to turn around and look back at me, pushing her fire-red hair out of her eyes to wink at me.

Ruby was already breathing deeply and snoring slightly, which only left The Brain to worry about. "Hey, Josh?"

"Yeah."

"I'ma go talk to Pinky really quick. Do me a favor and keep Ruby occupied when she wakes up."

"Uh, ok," he replied hesitantly.

The bathroom door was still cracked open when I got to it, and I pushed it open to find her sitting on the sink. Closing the door, I stepped in between her open legs.

"You didn't cum yet, did you?"

"No, I didn't. Could you help with that?"

Her response was to smile and grab my dick until she had it poking her right up against her pussy lips. Even from this position I could feel the steady throb and heat of her womanhood. She looked at me with those hazel eyes, drawing me into her aura, pushing my want to a desperate need.

"Fuck me," she whispered into my mouth as she kissed me. I complied fully and pushed my dick deep inside her, shuddering at the feeling of how tight and warm she was and loving how she wrapped her legs around my back. Her moans were instant and loud, making me wonder how long Ruby was gonna stay asleep.

"Shh!" I told her, kissing her harder and pumping inside her faster.

"Choke me!" she ordered, grabbing my hands and putting them around her neck. I hesitated at first, but the hunger in her eyes pushed all doubt from my mind as I wrapped my big hands around her delicate neck and began to squeeze.

"Harder," she rasped.

I did as I was told, tightening my grip slightly while giving her longer strokes that seemed to reach up into her stomach. I felt her orgasm in a powerful downpour just as I heard the door open. I tried to step away from her, but she had me trapped with her legs locked around me and her pussy squeezing my dick.

Ruby was standing in the doorway naked, holding her pistol, her eyes going back and forth between Pinky and myself. "Ruby," I said in what I hoped was a neutral tone.

"Why didn't you invite me?"

At first I thought she was being sarcastic, but the look she was giving me said she was serious. Picking Pinky up, I followed Ruby back into the bedroom, where I found Josh tied to a bed, gagged.

"What the?"

"Don't trip, Tae. He's into bondage," she said, putting the gun on the nightstand.

They had pulled the beds together, so I laid Pinky down next to The Brain, and Ruby climbed on top of him. "You ready?" she asked me.

"Let's ride," I told her, once again fucking Pinky.

For the next hour positions changed as much as partners and bodily fluids until we all finally collapsed in a heap of sweat. "Amazing," I said to Ruby, holding her close to me.

"Mmhmm," she agreed.

I started drifting off until I felt someone kissing my dick before trying to swallow it whole. Ruby was still resting peacefully in my arms, so that only left one person. The twinkle in her eyes was pure mischief, but I was down for it, and I intended to prove she couldn't break me.

Up and down her head dipped, taking all of my dick into her mouth as she massaged my balls with her hands. To my knowledge she had never been with a black dude, but she was showing me she could handle me in any way. I could taste the blood in my mouth from me biting my tongue, but I couldn't moan, scream, or move without waking Ruby. The problem was she was sucking my dick so good I didn't know how long I could hold out. My toes were already curling, but there was no getting away from her. I tried to signal she needed to stop, but she just kept going until I grabbed her hair and let my cum gush in her mouth and down her throat.

Just as she was pulling her head back upward, her body was ripped from mine and she flew into the wall, a roar louder than thunder following her. My mind registered what was happening immediately, and I rolled with Ruby off the bed, grabbing her pistol on the way down.

"Housekeeping!" someone shouted through the hole in the door that joined adjacent rooms.

Ruby's gun was a fully automatic 9mm, and I let it spray both the door and the walls on either side, enjoying every scream of pain I heard from the next room.

"We gotta move!" I yelled, continuing to let bullets rain as Ruby scrambled for clothes and Josh scooped up the still-bleeding Pinky. The shotgun blast had hit a good portion of her, but I wouldn't know how bad it was until the blood was cleaned up. "Fuck the clothes! Move!" I screamed at Ruby, pushing her toward the second story balcony window. There was no telling what awaited us in the hallway, so going outside seemed like the better option. The question that kept rattling around in my mind was where the fuck all the homies was at? As soon as I opened the balcony door that question was answered, because the whole parking lot was lit up like a sunrise.

"Here," Ruby said, shoving the Mossberg pump into my hand and reclaiming her pistol. "I'll cover you," she said, turning back toward the room as Josh came out holding a barely conscious Pinky. I could hear gunfire shredding the walls in between the hotel rooms, which meant time was almost up.

"Josh, I want you to toss her to me once I'm on the ground," I said, climbing over the railing. I picked my spot to land, dropped the shotgun next to it, and prayed my knee held up as I let go. As soon as my feet touched the earth, I rolled to my right and scooped my gun up, looking for anything near me. Our room was thankfully pushed back from the street and parking lot a little, so I had some bushes and shadows to use as cover.

It sounded like a war zone down there with the repeated gunfire and occasional screams, and I could hear sirens in the distance, which meant it was time to go. "Come on!" I yelled back up, expecting to see Josh and Pinky. I was left waiting for a minute, and then they appeared at the railing.

There's really no way to gently drop a person from two stories up, and I could see Josh's indecision from where I stood. "I got her, Josh. Come on!"

He held her over the rail, and then he just let her go suddenly. I caught her and stumbled back until I was sitting, and only then I realized he'd screamed before she ever got to me. When I looked back up, all I saw was the barrel of an AK-47 scanning, trying to lock in on my location, which only meant one thing.

The knowledge of what had happened made my heart hurt, but I had to bury that pain for the moment or get buried.

"Josh," Pinky croaked, blood coating the lips that had just brought me so much pleasure a short while ago.

"I got you," I told her, picking her up and stumbling around the side of the building to my car. I could only imagine how we looked: naked, covered in blood. But luckily no one was around to witness the sight of me running away like a coward.

I laid her across the backseat of my all-black 2040 918I BMW and left the shotgun next to her, rushing around to the front before the enemy spotted us. "Fingerprint recognition activate," I said, gripping the steering wheel and waiting while my car ran my prints to ensure I was the owner. It was times like this I was glad I paid the extra money for this feature, because it was the only way to start my car without the keys.

Moments later the 1200 horses roared to life, and I got one with the wind, needing to put as much distance as possible between me and what was happening behind me. The problem was I didn't know where to go, and Pinky needed a hospital, A.S.A.P.!

"Call Nana," I said, hating that she was the only one I could turn to in this moment, but I needed her.

The phone rang eight times before she finally picked up. "Hello?" she mumbled.

"Nana, I need help."

"What is it? What's wrong, Tae?"

"One of mine is shot, and I need a doctor before she bleeds to death."

"Where are you?"

"I'm in Virginia."

"Virginia! Okay, listen. Get her to Reston Hospital immediately. I'll have someone meet you there."

"Okay, okay."

"Baby, is it Ruby? Where's Ruby?"

"She's – Ruby's dead!"

Aryanna

Chapter 23

Kevin

2027

"Mom? Mom, are you here yet?" I called out, coming through the side door. It had been too many years since I had been in this house, but being on the w

I walked into my kitchen and turned on the overhead lights, illuminating my Spanish tiled floor and granite countertops. I took pride in my kitchen with its state-of-the-art cooking appliances and tasteful décor because I loved to cook. It was something my father passed on to me, and cooking made me feel closer to him.

I decided my mother would probably be starving after her long drive to Norfolk, so why not whip her up something? Business first, though.

Sitting at the center island that bisected the kitchen, I poured myself a shot of Hennessey and pulled out my phone. My call was answered on the second ring. "Everything okay?" I asked.

"Yes, sir. I'm still keeping her sedated, as you instructed, and there haven't been any problems."

"Good, good. I'm in town, and the time is near, so expect to see me soon."

"Yes, sir."

I disconnected the call just as a text message came in, but I didn't recognize the sending number. *Call me,* the text read. It was probably just somebody with the wrong number, so I put my phone to the side and started prepping my meal.

My mother was a hardworking woman, and she deserved to be pampered. And since no man was worth her time, that left the pampering to me. I didn't mind, though. Shit, she'd bought this six bedroom, four bath house for me on my eighteenth birthday, not to mention all the love she'd given me my entire life. There were so many mothers in the world today that didn't give a damn about their children, and I understood just how blessed I was to have had her. Especially after my dad was gone.

Looking in the freezer and refrigerator, I saw my instructions had been followed with regards to my food choices, which meant I needed to give my year-round maid a bonus. I selected both shrimp and steak, figuring surf and turf would put a smile on my mom's face, and hopefully a nice, normal dinner would lighten her mood.

I could understand her worry somewhat, but at the end of the day Devaughn Mitchell was a mortal that needed oxygen to survive, just like the rest of us. The nigga wasn't special. He was just lucky as a muthafucka.

Mom had insisted a little work would take her mind away from the chaos for a moment, and that's what she needed. Hopefully she was right and had gotten her peace of mind, because it was time to make Devaughn poke his head back out. He hadn't made a visible move in weeks, but he couldn't play dead for long. Not if he wanted his baby mama back. Of course, he wouldn't get her back, this was just my way of forcing him to show himself. It was actually surprising he hadn't made a move, but with the whole Blood nation likely on his ass too, there wasn't anywhere safe.

Or maybe he was dead, but that was just wishful thinking on my part.

I made a couple of loaded baked potatoes and tossed a salad to go with the main course. Once I'd selected a nice red wine to chill and set the table for two, I was ready, but Mom still wasn't here.

Picking up the phone, I saw I had a multimedia message, but I had no idea who'd be sending me a video. Pressing play, I saw my aunt Erica and her three kids sitting on their couch. Slowly the view changed. I saw her husband Snoop standing in between the couch and the loveseat, and sitting on the loveseat was my mother. The video's angle stopped rotating and went back to my aunt's husband, where it stopped. A pistol appeared in the scene and moved steadily toward him until a man was standing there, holding the gun to his forehead. Without hesitation, he pulled the trigger, and Snoop's body dropped.

That's when the screaming started.

My blood ran cold as the gun was turned on my aunt and cousins, but that didn't stop him from pulling the trigger. I couldn't see the man's face, but I knew it wasn't Devaughn.

When the children's screams faded, the silence in the room was thicker than the gun smoke, and I prayed it was over. But then the gun was turned on my mother. Suddenly Deshana's face swam into view and she spoke two words.

"Call me."

The screen went black, and I was left alone with the crazy real fear of becoming an orphan. I thought I'd covered my tracks, or at the very least I'd had more time before he found out who I was. The name and things I'd told Deshana had been lies, and my paperwork had been flawless, yet they still knew. At this point it didn't matter how they knew. What mattered was getting my mother back.

Numbly, I dialed the number from the text and listened to it ring for what seemed like an eternity.

"Hello," she sang, answering the phone.

"Don't hurt her."

"I don't want to. I didn't wanna hurt you or anyone in your family, but you came for mine," she replied seriously.

"Your father. This is all your father's fault!"

"You act like your father was innocent! That nigga had blood on his hands, too, and he tried to kill my father. He just wasn't good enough."

"Fuck you, bitch!"

"Oh, you did, but rest assured I'ma fuck you before it's over."

"Give me my mother."

"Fair exchange has never been a robbery."

"Where?"

"Virginia Beach, two hours," she replied, hanging up in my ear.

That meant I had one hour to figure out how to get to them and kill them. If not, we were dead!

Chapter 24

DJ

2040

If there was one thing I detested, it was the way my father would summon me to him. Granted this time he'd called it a family meeting, but there was never an option of not attending when the great Devaughn Mitchell wanted some face time. My best guess was that he'd seen the news, and now he was fed up enough to fight back. It was obvious he was losing as much money as he was sleep, because having his businesses targeted didn't exactly bring new investors to the table. Even I was smart enough to know that.

It was time to end this thing once and for all with Devonte. I should've never played the cat and mouse game from the beginning. I just knew my father wouldn't have sanctioned this war unless it was bought to his door. He tried not to show his ruthless side without provocation. Admittedly, I didn't see shit getting this far out of control to the point innocent kids were dying in the streets.

"DJ, you ready?" Deshana called from my living room. The time had come.

I shut down the computer system and lights and locked my door on the way out. I walked into the living room to find Brianna feeding little Hope and my big sister tapping her foot impatiently.

"Dad wants us now," she said.

"Let's go," I replied, making my way toward the front door.

"DJ?" Brianna called out. The look she gave me said she had something to say, but wanted us to talk in private.

"I'm coming," I said to Deshana, looking at her so she knew to proceed to the house without me. Turning back to Brianna, I sat across from her and waited for her to speak.

"Why did you show me the news? And why should I believe anything you said about Devonte, knowing that you hate him?"

"Because you needed to know, and because you know I'm not lying. But it's not about you."

"Oh yeah? What's it about, then?"

"It's about that beautiful little girl you're holding. I held her in my hands, and I felt her take her first breath and fight her way into this world. I feel responsible for her life, and this isn't the life I'd want for her, because she deserves a fair chance. She deserves to grow up without bodies falling all around her. She deserves a father that's not about that life, because that life claims whatever victims it can. My oldest sister died the same night my mother did. Her head was cut off. That blood is on Devonte's Mom's hands, but it's on my father's, too, because of the life he chose. In this life your own family will devour you. Now, is that what you want for Hope?"

I could see the fear in her eyes behind the tears sliding down her beautiful face. I could also see the understanding and the light in those hazel eyes that came from realizing she could only lie to herself for so long. I knew she needed to work this out for herself because I couldn't live her life for her. Plus, I had a meeting to get to. I stood up and placed a kiss on top of Hope's head before making my way back toward the door.

"DJ?"

"Yeah?"

"What life do I have without him? He's all I've known."

"Whatever you decide to do, I got you, my word."

The slight nod of her head let me know my word meant something to her, so now all I had to do was stay alive long enough to keep it.

Outside I ran into CJ, who had just pulled up and was unloading diapers from the car. "Hey, DJ."

"What's up, sexy?"

"Just doing my job. Where are you headed?"

"To a meeting with my dad, but I'll be back later on."

"Good, because I wanted to talk to you."

Her tone brought me up short and made me stop in front of her. "What's up?" I asked, searching her green eyes intently.

"It's just, um. Well, what happened between us ain't something I normally do. Mixing business with pleasure always ends up bad."

"But you made that exception for me, huh?" I asked, taking her hands in mine. Her smile was a brilliant white, and she blushed a deep red before meeting my gaze. "What is it you really want, CJ?"

"I just want you to be real with me, because that's the only way I'ma respect you. I'm not asking for broken promises. I'm a big girl that knows how the world works. I–"

I silenced her by leaning down and kissing her tenderly, pulling her closer until I had her tiny frame molded to my body. I knew she was trying to tell me not to play with her heart, but I wanted to tell her she didn't have to worry about that. "I know you're a good girl, sweetheart, and I won't lie to you and tell you I'm not something like a bad boy. What I will tell you is that I'm not gonna hurt you, and I'ma keep shit honest, no matter what."

"I'm glad you feel that way, because I need to be honest with you about something."

I felt the black cloud of doom lurking, but there was no way to avoid what she wanted to say. "Alright, what is it?"

"I-I have a daughter."

"Okay. And?"

"I just need you to know that. I'm not with her father anymore, and I don't know how you feel about kids, but you're absolutely wonderful with Hope. Not that I'm asking you to be a father to mine, I just—"

"Shh!" I told her, putting my finger to her lips. "It's beautiful that you're a single mother handling her business, and when the time is right, I'd love to meet your little girl, okay?"

"Okay. Are you sure?"

"Yes, I'm sure. Right now I have to go to this meeting, though, so can we finish this conversation later?"

"Sure, I'll be here."

"Okay," I told her, kissing her one more time before I let her go. When the time was right, I definitely planned to get to know her better. She was cool as shit, plus the pussy was fire!

I quickly made my way to the main house and into my father's conference room. "Took you long enough," he said.

I didn't respond, just took my seat next to Deshana. In attendance at this family meeting was my sister's wife, JuJu, and my dad's wife, Belinda. I was surprised that no foot soldiers were here because I'd fully expected this to be a meeting to discuss strategy. The only thing that was obvious was that something was wrong. "Well, Dad, you've got the family together, except for Bella and Day-Day," I commented.

"At this time Isabella's grandfather and I have decided it's best for her to go back to Italy until all of this is settled, and Sharday is out on tour, but she's aware of what it is," he said.

"Any change from Ramona?" Deshana asked. We were all hoping one day she'd awaken from her coma, but after more than a decade we understood it was only hope. She still had brain function and she was a fighter, plus she was getting all the help money could buy.

We had all dealt with the loss of her in our own way, but it had hurt me deeper than anyone because I'd lost two mothers. In a lot of ways those losses had turned my heart cold, but the love and attention JuJu had showed me helped to heal me a little at a time. I, in turn, had helped heal my baby sister Bella, because she'd never known her mother outside of talking to her in a coma. No one knew what that was like, but I did. Bella was all my father had left of his first love, so I could understand him wanting to protect her, and his anger at my irresponsible actions.

"No change from her, but I know Bella and her are safe," he replied. "Right now my focus is on keeping the rest of you safe and ending this bullshit once and for all."

"How, Dad?" I asked.

His response was to look directly at Deshana, and somehow I knew this conversation was one they'd had before.

"Are you sure, Dad?" she asked.

"Yeah, baby, I am. The truce ended the moment they thought using my son was a good idea."

"What truce, Dad? And what the fuck do you mean *your son*?" I asked, baffled by him suddenly claiming Devonte.

"First of all, don't take that tone with me, because I'll break your muthafuckin' face, boy! Now, some years ago I made a deal with the head Bloods up top that we'd just go our separate ways and leave each other alone because it wasn't good business to do otherwise. They agreed, and that should've been the end of it, but them sucking Devonte into their world shows this was their end play all along. And I called Devonte my son because that's exactly what he is." He held up his hand to stop my protest before I could utter a word.

"I just found out my father wasn't really my biological father, which means Keyz and I don't share the same blood. Which means Devonte wasn't born from incest, and he's as much my son as you, DJ. I owe him—"

"That's bullshit! You don't owe him a goddamn thing!" I raged, not caring how my father felt about the tone I was using.

"He's telling the truth, DJ," Belinda said. "I was there when he found out, and I beat the truth out of his step mother just to make sure."

My mind was racing at a speed I couldn't control, and my emotions were in hot pursuit. That nigga would never be a brother of mine, never.

"The only way to end this war is to go after the puppet master, so that's our next move. Deshana, I want you to make the call," he said. My sister nodded her head in the affirmative, but I could feel her eyes on me.

I couldn't believe what I was hearing. I didn't give a fuck about the bloods, they were just a bonus in this fight. Whether my father was related to Devonte's mom or not, he still should've never been born! He had to die.

"So, that's it? The great Devaughn has spoken, and we're to obey your command?" I asked sarcastically.

"Son, I know you're hurt."

"If you know how hurt I am, then tell me vengeance is mine to have."

His mouth opened, but not a single word passed his lips. I'd never seen the man speechless before.

"Just like I thought," I told him, getting up and opening the door. I walked away without a backward glance, my heart heavier than I could ever remember it being, because for the first time I didn't feel like my father's son.

I went straight back to my house, my mind made up on what had to be done next and eager to get started. As soon as I was in my office, I hit the link to 3D face time with The Mad Hacker.

"What's up, DJ?" he asked.

"Find him now, Evy! He has to be down here in Virginia because of all the moves being made against us, and I wanna know where he's at."

"I'm on it," he replied, disappearing.

"Can I come in?" Deshana asked from the door. I nodded my head and she came in and took one of the seats in front of my desk. "I get i. I felt the same way about his mom when I thought she'd killed dad. But DJ, I promise you this plan we set in motion is gonna work."

"Work for who, Lil' M? My mother is gone, and now my own father basically wants me to let that go without my piece of flesh. Am I not owed that much, or do I just matter that little?"

"Come on, DJ, don't even think like that. Dad loves you, but the situation is impossible! He can't kill one of his own children, let alone sanction you to do it."

"So I'm just supposed to let it go, huh?"

I expected her to say yeah, but instead she said nothing. I may have been my father's junior, but she was more like him than anyone, and right then I could see that analytical mind working.

"You sure you want this? You want this type of blood on your hands?"

From anybody else I would've answered this question without hesitation, but with her I had to be damn sure. I knew what my big sister was capable of and how bloody her hands really were, just like I knew it wasn't easy for her to live with all she'd done. It had been years since my oldest sister, La-La, was murdered, as well as their sister Jordyn, but Deshana still carried the guilt. A guilt like that could destroy someone, but losing all I'd already lost destroyed my belief in a life that made sense without the justice I deserved.

"I can handle it," I told her confidently.

"Okay, lil' bruh, let me make some calls," she replied, standing up and leaving the room.

As soon as she walked out, Brianna walking in, carrying a very fussy Hope in her arms. "Not now, Bri!"

"She's cranky as fuck and she won't go to sleep for me or CJ."

"Not now."

She ignored what I said and put little Hope right in my arms. The miracle of the situation was she got quiet immediately, much to the annoyance of her mother. "That's some straight bullshit, son! My daughter loves you more than me!"

I didn't say anything, but it was hard not to smile at the beautiful, brown-skinned, hazel-eyed bundle in my arms. I sat there and rocked her for all of five minutes before she was out cold. CJ came through and took her to the nursery, leaving me and Brianna alone.

"You obviously have something to say, so say it, because I gotta get to work," I told her.

"Did you mean what you said about helping me?"

"I wouldn't have said it if I didn't mean it."

She got quiet again, but I didn't rush her to talk because I could see the heavy thought she was in.

My computer made the familiar buzzing noise that came with an incoming message before The Mad Hacker popped up on my screen. "Found him," he said without preamble.

My eyes locked with Brianna as I waited on her decision, not needing her permission, but wondering where her loyalties lay. "Send the info to my car," I replied never taking my eyes off of her. A silence that spoke a thousand words filled the room, but I wasn't gonna be the one to break it.

Finally she stood up from the seat she'd taken and walked around the desk to stand in front of me. Still looking deep into my eyes, she leaned down and pressed her juicy lips to my own, opening her mouth and allowing me to taste the sweet watermelon flavored Kool-Aid on her tongue.

Her kiss had me pinned to my chair, but before I knew it, it was over. "Thank you!" she said, pulling back and turning for the door. I felt my tongue still in my mouth, but I couldn't think of a word to say.

After ten minutes of heavy breathing, I got my shit together enough to call Deshana. "I know where he is. I want his blood on my hands."

Aryanna

Chapter 25

Devaughn Sr.

2027

Now that I knew who the boogieman was, it was time to bring him to his knees. Murdaheart had provided what little info he had to give, but I knew someone who was guaranteed to know a lot more.

"Deshana, Fish, C-note, JuJu: get your homies ready, because it's time to make some shit happen," I told them, pulling out my own phone to make a call.

He answered immediately, and I could hear the stress in his voice. "Mr. Petras, it's Devaughn."

"Hello, son. What can I do for you?"

"How's my wife?"

"She's – She's still with us. You know Ramona is a helluva fighter, and she won't give up. The doctor's say there is still some brain activity despite the blood and oxygen loss she suffered."

"What are her chances?"

"I do not rely on numbers. I know the strength of my daughter, and I know she will come back to us."

I prayed he was right. We had so little time together, and we deserved so much more. It was still hard to swallow that she was in this condition by the hand of my own mother, but that was a truth better left unsaid to this man. "Please keep me updated."

"I will, son. She loved you very much," he said, his voice breaking slightly.

I couldn't express fully how much I loved her too, but there would be time to grieve for what we'd lost. Now was the time to settle all scores. I updated him on all that was happening, including my plans for the ultimate takeover.

"You know I never really respected the whole gang scene, but you have a mind very different from the average. Explain to me how this will play out," he said.

"It starts with having young Crips without records go to work as correctional officers in the prisons in upstate New York where the Bloods' upper echelon are incarcerated. Once they are in place, we take a group of Crips and educate them on how to be an east coast Blood, giving them the cover they need to survive Riker's Island and make it to actual prison. We do this until we have enough Crips posing as Bloods to eliminate the entire hierarchy when they receive the order."

"So you're taking the mentality of a terrorist sleeper cell and implemented it on gangbanging warfare?" he asked, somewhat puzzled.

"More or less," I replied.

The silence hummed on the line for a minute before he spoke again. "Genius," he remarked, clearly impressed. "So what is it you need from me?"

"Right now I need to infiltrate Holford Trucking Company so I can tie up some loose ends. I need a location on its owner. Can you help?"

"Let me make a call. I will be in touch," he replied, disconnecting.

If anybody could find out anything without the target knowing they were looking, it'd be him and his family. The mob may not have been a dominant as it once was in the public eye, but the best trick the devil ever pulled was convincing the world he didn't exist.

"We're ready, Dad," Deshana said once everyone was off the phone. It was time to get back to business and once again make the streets fear my wrath.

"I'm waiting on a location on Kevin's mom, and when that comes in we'll move against her in order to get to him. I don't know if they thought we couldn't or wouldn't find them, but we're gonna make some house calls tonight. Butta, I want you with me because we're gonna pay a visit to Skino's sister and get some answers. The rest of you load up and follow us."

We all moved out and piled into two black Denalis, moving through the city streets with the speed and determination of the president's motorcade. The last time I'd made the run into the seven cities of Virginia it had been to pick up my traitorous big homie, and there I was five years later going after his family. When would it end? When would I be able to put the predator in me to the side and just be a man about his family? Sometimes I felt like I been in a war my entire life, because I was so tired of fighting. But with death being the only option, fighting for life was what I had to do. I knew this wouldn't be my last fight, but if I did this the right way, I could assure myself that when the end came, me and mine would be the last ones standing.

I felt my phone going off and pulled it from my pocket to answer. "Hello?"

"I have the information you requested, and my men are already picking her up."

"Thank you, Mr. Petras."

"You are welcome. Where would you like her delivered?"

"I know the perfect spot, one fitting for a night of long overdue justice. I want her in the trunk of a car parked across the street from the Norfolk State University. Just let me know what kind of car it is and the license plate."

"I will use one of her cars, and I will send you all the information you require."

"Thank you!"

"I'm doing this favor for you, but I must ask a favor in return."

"Ok," I said warily. I didn't know how I could possibly help him, but whatever it was had to be major. "Tell me, how much time did you get to spend with Ramona before? Before she was shot?"

"Very little. I'd just woken up into this nightmare of being under siege. I mean, I literally opened my eyes to the sounds of gunfire in my house."

"So you and her didn't really have a chance to talk?"

"No. Why?"

"Well because – because she was pregnant."

"Pregnant?" I asked, completely dumbstruck. I knew Ramona couldn't have kids because we had that conversation early on. It had made telling her about DJ that much harder. Yet somehow she'd gotten pregnant by some other nigga while I laid in a coma? I knew I had no right to feel the anger and betrayal that I did, especially with the way I had betrayed her with other women, but the tightness in my chest told me my emotions were very real. "How?" I asked, needing some type of sense to be made of what was just told to me."

"Invitro fertilization. She went to a clinic in Akron, Ohio and had it done. She was so happy to be having a little girl."

"Who's the father?" I asked around the lump in my throat.

"You are!"

"But how? That can't be, because—"

"If you know anything about my daughter, you know how determined she is when she wants something. And you know how much she loved you."

I knew his words were those of truth, but instead of celebrating, all I could do was cry silent tears at losing another daughter on top of all I'd already lost. "I'm sorry. I'm so sorry, Mr. Petras."

"You need not be. You see, the baby lives on inside Ramona even as she remains unconscious. When the time is right, she will be able to give birth and all will be well, I'm told."

"My baby? My baby will live?"

"Yes!"

I felt the vise grip that had ahold of my heart loosen just a little with that one word, and I began to feel the joy of knowing a little miracle had been created between me and the woman I loved so much. But why was he just now telling me this?

"I'm sure your analytical mind is wondering why I didn't share this information with you sooner, and I will explain. Your life is not one safe to bring a child into at the moment, and I think you're man enough to agree. However, I know my daughter wouldn't want you separated from your child. The favor I ask of you now is that you allow my grandchild to be raised here until it's safe for her to be around you. I encourage you to come out here whenever you feel the need, but please allow her to stay in my country for now."

I knew his request was coming from a place of love, and it was a love of family I'd yearned for my entire life. He was right: I was man enough to see my baby being with me right now wasn't a good look, but I wanted her so bad. As a parent, we sometimes have to make the decisions that are unbearably hard, though, and this was one of those times. "Keep them safe," I said, wiping the tears from my face.

"Indeed I will, son. I look forward to seeing you, son, so take care of what you have to out there. Just be safe and smart, because you have a lot of people who love and need you."

"Understood," I replied, hanging up.

The next few hours passed in a blur of mayhem, only slowing down when I saw him exit his house. No doubt he thought he had time to find out where we were with his mother and ambush us, but he didn't realize chess masters only became victorious when they could see ten moves ahead of their opponent.

"Hello, Kevin," I said from behind him, chambering a fresh round into the barrel of my pistol. He was smart enough to freeze, but I could feel the tension rolling off him. "Did you know that a Glock has no safety, Kevin? So if you think you have time to do anything short of farting before I blow the front of your skull out, you should reconsider. Where's my baby's mama?" I asked, jamming the gun to the base of his skull.

He didn't answer me, and that was okay. He'd talk, though. They all talked in the end.

"Move!" I ordered, smacking him with the pistol and pushing him toward his backyard. The good thing about having money is it afforded you privacy, so this secluded, fenced-in backyard seemed like the best place to talk without witnesses.

As we moved further into the gloom, I heard a familiar sound I knew the young boy in front of me wouldn't recognize if his life depended on it. The closer we got to the northwest corner of the yard, the more recognizable the figures standing there became, as well as the mountain of dirt that came from the hole C-note was digging.

"Want me to perform the last rights?" Butta asked, laughing.

"He don't deserve them," I said, pushing him toward the giant hole in the ground. "Bind his legs and feet," I told Deshana.

For a moment she didn't move, just stared at him with a hatred so bright I thought it would light the night sky. "Where's my mother?" she all but whispered at him.

His response was a smile, which was the absolute wrong thing for him to do. Had he known Deshana as well as he thought he did, he would've seen the blow coming, but because he didn't, he took a knee flush to his nuts. Once he was down, she bound his hands and feet, and then proceeded to kick every tooth out of his mouth that she could. C-note and Fishback eventually pulled her off of him, but it was too soon in my opinion.

"I could think of a thousand ways to kill you, and you deserve them all. But does your mother? Think of the unspeakable torture I'm gonna put her through because of you. I wish your father were alive to tell you what a blowtorch to your balls will do for honesty, but take my word as the gospel when I tell you it ain't pretty. What do you think I'ma do to your mom?"

I could see the anger in his eyes, in the set of his jaw, but then he smiled. "You probably can't do any worse than I did to your daughter, you bitch muthafucka. Her pussy made a nice fire extinguisher for a road flare I just happened to have," he said, laughing.

I felt the cold sweep over me, and I knew my daughters' mother might forever be lost to us, because he had to die. Now! Grabbing him by his throat, I dragged him to the hole and was prepared to throw him down it when his phone started ringing. I searched until I found it, and when I did I knew the spirit of my daughter was with me. The caller, whomever she was, had sent a text first asking if she should give "her" another sedative or wait until Kevin arrived.

"We got what we need right here. Bury that bitch," I told C-note.

Taking my daughter's hand, I walked with her back to the truck where JuJu was posted, watching for any other help lil' nigga might've had. "You ok, Lil' M?" I asked.

"I feel so stupid, Dad. I mean, how did I not know for all these years?"

"Baby girl, you were grieving and vulnerable. You can't blame yourself for not seeing what he did so well."

"But Dad."

"He's right, Deshana. You're forgetting I was there with you, too, and I didn't see it."

I watched the two of them exchange a look of more than just words, but the love they felt for each other was plain to see.

"What now, Dad?"

"First we go get your mother, and then—"

I was interrupted by my own phone buzzing, alerting me of a text message that said Skino's widow was now in the trunk of a car in front of NSU, and they wanted to know if I needed anything else. My message was a simple three words: Blow it up.

"And after we get Mom?" Deshana asked.

"Well, then we begin the takeover," I said, sending the video of Murdaheart to the secretary of the council. Just as it was with Murdaheart, their ass was mine.

Chapter 26

DJ

2040

I was the second one through the hotel room door, covering Deshana while looking for Devonte's lifeless corpse. To my disappoint, the nigga was nowhere in sight, but the naked bitch my sister was holding at gunpoint could probably shed some light on his location.

"Where is he?" I asked, pointing my gun at her head.

"Fuck you!" she said, trying to spit in my face.

I didn't have time to respond before Deshana backhanded her with the pistol, knocking her to the floor.

"Take her. She'll answer our questions sooner or later," I said, hearing the sirens in the distance.

Deshana grabbed her by her hair and pulled her to her feet. "Fight me and you die right here," she warned.

I could see the fight in the woman's eyes, but I could also see the wisdom it took to understand we weren't playing. We made it out of the hotel and to the parking lot without having to exchange any more gunfire, but there was no sign of that slippery muthafucka Devonte.

"Put her in the back of the truck and tell your soldiers to load up," I told Deshana, climbing behind the wheel of my car. "Call Evy. I need you to find him, because he can't be that far."

"I watched it from the hotel footage. He's in a black BMW and he was carrying some girl with him. If she's not dead, then he's looking for a hospital, and from your location that only leaves two options: Fairfax and Reston."

"Which way was he headed?"

"They're both in the same direction, heading northeast from Centerville."

"Okay, I'ma go to Reston Hospital. I want you to send the message to my sister to go to Fairfax Hospital after she stashes the package in a safe house. I want you to hack into both hospital surveillance databases and monitor them so we don't miss him. His ass dies tonight!"

***

Devaughn Sr.

"Devaughn? Devaughn, wake up! Your mother is on the phone."

Her voice came from far away, and what she just said sounded like a bad dream. My mother knew better than to call me, and with the shit I'd just learned, this was the absolute wrong time to talk to me. The clock on my nightstand said it was 3:45 a.m., and only bad news came at this time of the morning. "What?" I grumbled once I'd grabbed the phone from Belinda.

"Devaughn, wake up. Please, it's important!"

I hadn't heard her voice in thirteen years, but I'd know it anywhere. Just like I'd know the blind panic pushing the words out of her mouth at a rapid fire pace. "Slow down, slow down. What's wrong?" I asked, sitting up and swinging my feet over the side of the bed.

"Devonte's in trouble! He's down there in Virginia, and something has happened because he said his best friend is dead. Devaughn, what did you do?"

"Do? I ain't did shit! I ain't pushed back against him because I just found out his mother may not have been my sister after all."

The silence that followed my statement was the loudest of my life. I never dreamed my mother could tell a lie this big or kept it going for almost half a century, but she didn't even offer a rebuttal. The feeling of my wife's hand rubbing my back gave me the comfort I didn't even know I needed. I couldn't express the hurt at being robbed of a father because the one I had was a P.O.S. I didn't even wanna think about how different my life could've been. In that moment I understood how different my children's lives deserved to be.

"Where is he?"

"I sent him to Reston Hospital and called Tiffany to meet him."

"What happened?"

"All I know is that his best friend Ruby is dead, and another of his people is shot."

Tiffany Marie was my mother's sister-in-law, and she was a nurse, which meant she could help them get in and out without having to report the gunshot wound to the cops. "Tiffany can handle it."

"Devaughn, he needs you! And you need to tell your people to back off!"

"My people haven't made a move because I haven't told them to. He's got more enemies than me."

"Where's DJ?"

My immediate response was to say he was sleeping like most normal people at this time, but DJ wasn't normal. He was my son. And he wanted revenge. "I'll call you back," I told my mother, already putting my sweatpants and Timbs on.

"I'm coming with you," Belinda said, getting up.

"No, I need you here. Call Deshana and tell her to meet me at Reston Hospital," I said, grabbing my keys and my pistol before heading out the door. I had a bad feeling about this, because DJ had more of me in him than I liked, and I knew what I'd do in this situation.

"DJ!" I screamed, unlocking his door and going toward the stairs. "DJ!"

"He's not here," she said from the living room.

I followed her voice into the darkness and found Brianna sitting on the couch, the moonlight twinkling off the tears that lined her cheeks. "Where is he?" I asked, knowing the answer.

"Him and his sister went after Tae."

I felt the knot in my stomach tighten, because with Deshana by his side, they wouldn't stop until they got their man. "Fuck!" I said, turning around to go out the door.

"I'm coming with you."

"Okay, it might help Devonte to know you're safe."

"I'm not going for Devonte," she replied.

I didn't know what that meant. All I knew was I had to find Tae before DJ did.

***

2027

The war had been raging for six months, at times getting so hectic that grocery shopping could shorten one's life expectancy. The southern states like Georgia, Alabama, Tennessee, and Florida hadn't been hard to take over since Blood presence wasn't that high, but moving north had been a battle. Headline after headline was made, eventually causing the local and national law enforcement agencies to band together. That didn't stop me, though, because this war had to be realized in order for my family to ever know peace. My strategy was simple: take no prisoners.

The response from the video of Murdaheart's rape had been exactly what I expected it to be. I had done it for the humiliation factor, but also to recall the Bloods' despised Raymond Washington and other Crips back in the '60s because they felt like rape was a crime beneath them.

There were no rules to war. The objective was to break your opponent both mentally and physically until fighting back wasn't an option. Murdaheart had been the beginning of my mental warfare, but it didn't stop there. To date I have recorded eight videos of different big homies being fucked in their ass by the dragon slayer Happy Jack. Was I sick for taking a perverse pleasure in this part of the battle? Without question. But they should've thought of that before they came fucking with me.

My latest efforts of running the Bloods out of Virginia had been going well enough for me to feel comfortable having my daughter's wedding on the site of what would be our new house. It was hard to believe my little girl, my Mini Me, was getting married. But I approved of her relationship with JuJu. She was a good woman and I knew she loved Deshana, and that was all that mattered at this point. Her mother was there with us, and we were gonna give our baby away together. I wished Ramona and Candy were there. They loved Deshana so much.

And JuJu? I couldn't say enough about her. She was amazing, especially when it came to DJ and being what he needed right now to get through this storm. I wish he didn't understand as much as he did, but it was beyond my power to undo what had been done. Sadly, he was another statistic: a child whose innocence was snatched way before his time. I'd give anything to give him that back.

"Daddy?" he said, walking over to where I was sitting on the hood of my truck watching everyone prepare for the wedding.

"What's up, lil' man?" I said, hopping down and scooping him up in my arms.

"Whatcha doing?"

"I was just sitting here thinking about you. What are you doing?"

"I was thinking about Mommy. She would like how pretty my big sister is."

"Yeah, she would," I said, swallowing the tears I wanted to shed.

"I miss Mommy and Mona, Daddy. Can't I see Mona like I saw you every day?" he asked earnestly.

"It's not that easy, DJ, because she lives with her daddy now, and that's a long way from here. We'll go visit her soon, though. I promise."

He just shook his little head, pushing dreads out of his face. I knew he had so many questions I'd never have answers for, but I'd always love him the best I could.

"Daddy?"

"Yeah, lil' man?"

"I know what happened to Mommy."

I didn't know what to say to that statement. He'd seen his mother murdered, so it wasn't like I could make it any better for him by lying. "I know, DJ."

"When I grow up, I'ma do the same thing that was done to her, but I'ma do it to everybody who hurt us," he said.

Most parents might've passed off that statement as nonsense, nothing more than an emotional child. But they couldn't see the look in his eyes. They couldn't look to their child and see a reflection of their torment in his young face.

But I could.

Chapter 27

Devonte

2040

In my short eighteen years of life, I'd never known rage and fear to battle so hard for control in my body. My fear was for the future, because without Ruby so much was unknown. I mean, she was my right arm. How could I win the war without her?

So was I forced to accept the loss of my wife and baby, too? I could never accept that. Never!

My fear was also for Pinky. She'd still been unconscious when I got her to the hospital, and they'd rushed her into surgery, but they hadn't been out to tell me anything. My rage was for the loss of Ruby, too. That shit couldn't go unchecked. My father and brother would pay for that, and blood was the only even trade.

I couldn't stop my hands from shaking, and my thoughts kept jumping around so much it was making me dizzy. I couldn't seem to get warm. I had a spare sweat suit and shoes, along with the black-on-black Glock .19 with laser sight Ruby had given me for my birthday in my trunk, but I didn't feel safe or warm. I felt vulnerable. I felt like I'd been exposed, like my gangsta had been tried, and I'd failed miserably.

I could only imagine what the big homies up top were saying and thinking right then, but I couldn't let that worry me at the moment. My mind was on what had to be done in that moment, because the next one wouldn't matter if I wasn't alive to experience it.

I pulled my phone from my pocket again and tried to call Noodles to make contact with the council. They needed to be informed about Ruby, because someone had to break the news to the family, but nobody was answering. I hung up and called my grandma instead.

"Nana?"

"Are you okay, Tae?"

"I'm fine, it's Pinky that's in surgery."

"How is she?"

"I don't know. I'm waiting in the ER for someone to tell me something. Why is no one up there answering the phone?"

"You don't need to worry about that. Just take care of Pinky and come home."

"Come home? I'm not going no-fucking-where without my wife and kid! And it's no way in hell I'm letting them get away with killing Ruby!"

"Tae, please! Please come home before I lose you, too."

"You won't lose me, Nana. Just get in touch with Noodles and get the homies to send everybody they can down here."

"No one's coming, Tae."

"Huh? Of course they'll come. This war was sanctioned from Mr. Billy Bad Ass himself. And there's no way Ruby's death will go unanswered."

"Baby, listen to me. There's no one left. They're dead."

"What do you mean there's no one left? You're not making any sense right now."

"I know you haven't seen the news, so I'll explain it as best as I can. Sometime yesterday all the big homies, the originators of the movement, were killed. I know how impossible that sounds, but I swear to you it's true. A war has broken out, and what Bloods remain are now running for their lives. The Crips own New York, baby. It's over."

I heard her words, but it was like she was speaking Martian or something, because the shit wasn't making sense. Crips didn't have numbers or an interest in New York. I mean, it was the birthplace of the east coast movement. That was like Bloods trying to take over Jordan Downs out in Cali, or trying to erase Grape Street from existing. It was impossible.

"That could never happen," I said, wishing I sounded more confident.

"Baby, I wouldn't lie to you. Not about this. Come home, please. I promise you will get Brianna with the baby back safely."

I hung up the phone, needing to think without her voice in my ear. The more sense I tried to make of what she'd just told me, the less sense it made. No one Blood was invincible, but the united Blood nation had to be, didn't it?

"Who's here for Amber Lucille?" a short, dark haired female doctor asked.

"I am," I said, standing up and crossing to where the doctor stood. "How is she?"

"She's critical, but alive, and lucky as hell that it was buckshot instead of a slug."

"When can I see her?"

"It won't be tonight, but Tiffany told me you're family, so I can promise you that you'll see her tomorrow."

"Can you tell her I'm out here, Doc, so she knows she's not alone? Please!"

"She's still pretty much out of it. She lost a lot of blood, and it took some heavy drugs to make her comfortable. I'll do what I can, though."

I nodded my head in understanding before she walked away to leave me with my thoughts once again. I needed fresh air, and since it was obvious I wasn't gonna see Pinky anytime soon, it was time to leave.

The only problem was I had nowhere to go. The family I'd known, that had raised me, was all but gone, so who did I have left? Where did I belong in the world? I hadn't felt that alone since the day my mother didn't come back to get me, but with that thought in mind, I knew what to do. Family or no family, army behind me or not, I needed to go get Brianna and the baby, because without them I was just as good as dead.

With my mind made up, I started down the hall, but the sight of her pulled me up short. She was walking toward me like I'd conjured her from my mind, her tone legs as long as I remembered and making her overall thickness undeniable. Our baby girl hadn't hurt her at all based on the way her shorts were hugging her curves and how flat her stomach was underneath her baby doll t-shirt. Her black curls swayed with her purposeful stride, and her cinnamon brown skin glowed under the florescent lighting. She was as beautiful as the first day I'd seen her.

I saw the tears in her eyes before I noticed she'd stopped walking, but it didn't matter because I was moving toward her. I didn't notice him until we were a few feet apart, and although I'd never seen him face-to-face, it was obvious who he was.

"Hello, son," he said quietly.

For eighteen years I'd wondered what I would say to this man when we had this encounter. For eighteen years I'd heard his phantom voice in my mind saying the exact words he'd just spoken. And now that we were in the moment, I couldn't force all I wanted to say from my mouth.

The good thing was my grandma had taught me actions spoke louder than words, because with no thought required my pistol materialized in my hand.

"Tae, don't," she said, moving in front of my father.

"Move, Brianna. Move out the fucking way!"

"Tae, please! Just listen to him first."

"There's no talking, ma. He gotta die, and then it can be over."

"It'll never be over until you know the truth, sweetheart," she replied, crying openly now.

I didn't know what lies he'd told her, but I wasn't interested in the bullshit. "Move, Brianna," I said as calmly as I could.

"Tae, listen to me since you don't wanna listen to him. Your mother and him weren't related. He just found that out, and since then he's been trying to do everything he can to stop the war."

"Does that include killing my family and Ruby?"

At this question she turned to face him, looking for an explanation.

"If you're talking about anything that happened tonight, I promise you I didn't do it or sanction it. And the Bloods ain't your family. They are only loyal as long as you're doing what they want. They will chew you up and spit you out. Think about it, how many conflicts have you been in over the years? And how many have been with other Bloods? There's so much turmoil within, son, and it'll destroy you if you let it. I couldn't let that happen."

His words of concern meant shit to me, and I couldn't let that slide. "Move out the goddamn way, Brianna!" I yelled.

I felt the hot breeze of a bullet blow past my face before it embedded itself in the wall. The sound following it was no more than a whisper.

"DJ, don't!" I heard my father yell before him and Brianna stepped in front of me.

"Dad, move," he said, still trying to line up a clear shot on me while I was doing the same to him.

"You two are brothers, DJ. You're family, and that's what matters above all the bullshit the streets have to offer. Put the gun away."

"Dad, move!" he yelled again.

"Boy, put that goddamn gun down now! I'm not asking you, I'm telling you," our father replied.

"So the death of my mother goes unavenged? All that was taken from me is just something I'm expected to live with?" he asked, tears clouding his eyes that looked so much like my own.

"Don't you see that we've all lost, son? That there are no winners in this game as long as we're dealing in death? You and your brother have your whole lives in front of you to be much more than what your environment and experiences have made you, but only if it all ends now."

"Listen to him, DJ," Brianna said, taking steps toward him.

"Brianna, don't," I said.

She didn't even look back at me. She just continued walking until she was standing eye-level with his pistol.

"Bri. Bri, move. You know this has to end now. There's no other way," he said to her.

"And it will end now, but not like this, DJ. Now is the time for you to be that man I know you are. Now is the time for you to be the man Hope can be proud of and look up to."

A look I didn't understand passed from him to her, and I found myself wishing I could see her eyes.

"Brianna, get out of the way and away from him," I told her.

At first I thought she heard me because she began moving, but instead of moving toward me she put her back to him and took his hand in hers locking their fingers together. "What the? What the fuck?" I asked, feeling like I'd just had the wind knocked out of me.

"Put the gun down, DJ. This is the last time I'ma tell you," our father said.

"Do you remember the promise I made you, Dad, not long after Mom and Ramona got shot? Do you remember? I told you I was gonna do the same thing that was done to her to everyone who'd hurt us. You taught me to be a man of my word."

I wasn't sure if my father saw the look in his eyes, but I did, because I'd seen it before. It wasn't the look of defeat. It was determination.

I pulled the trigger a half a second after flames leapt from the barrel of his pistol and our father's head exploded. My first shot hit him high, and I had to adjust my sights, hoping one bullet would penetrate both Brianna and him. I felt an incredible burning in my chest that stood me straight up against the wall, but I kept squeezing the trigger.

As I felt myself slump to the floor, I took with me the satisfaction that not ten feet away from me, Brianna was slumped over DJ's body on the same linoleum. The last thing I heard were her wails and pleas for him not to die.

And I smiled.

To Be Continued...
A Gangster's Revenge 4
Coming Soon

Coming Soon From Lock Down Publications

RESTRAINING ORDER

By **CA$H & Coffee**

NO LOYALTY NO LOVE

By **CA$H & Reds Johnson**

GANGSTA SHYT

By **CATO**

PUSH IT TO THE LIMIT

By **Bre' Hayes**

GANGSTA CITY **II**

By **Teddy Duke**

BLOOD OF A BOSS **III**

By **Askari**

SHE DON'T DESERVE THE DICK

SILVER PLATTER HOE **III**

By **Reds Johnson**

BROOKLYN ON LOCK **III**

By **Sonovia Alexander**

THE STREETS BLEED MURDER **III**

By **Jerry Jackson**

CONFESSIONS OF A DOPEMAN'S DAUGHTER **III**

By **Rasstrina**

NEVER LOVE AGAIN **II**

WHAT ABOUT US **III**

By **Kim Kaye**

A GANGSTER'S REVENGE **IV**

By **Aryanna**

GIVE ME THE REASON **II**

By **Coco Amoure**

LAY IT DOWN **II**

By **Jamaica**

I LOVE YOU TO DEATH

By Destiny J

Available Now

LOVE KNOWS NO BOUNDARIES **I II & III**

By **Coffee**

SILVER PLATTER HOE **I & II**

HONEY DIPP **I & II**

CLOSED LEGS DON'T GET FED **I & II**

A BITCH NAMED KOCAINE

NEVER TRUST A RATCHET BITCH **I & II**

By **Reds Johnson**

A DANGEROUS LOVE **I, II, III, IV, V, VI, VII**

By **J Peach**

CUM FOR ME

An **LDP Erotica Collaboration**

A GANGSTER'S REVENGE **I & II**

By **Aryanna**

WHAT ABOUT US **I & II**

NEVER LOVE AGAIN

By **Kim Kaye**

THE KING CARTEL **I, II & III**

By **Frank Gresham**

BLOOD OF A BOSS **I & II**

By **Askari**

THE DEVIL WEARS TIMBS **I, II & III**

BURY ME A G **I II & III**

By **Tranay Adams**

THESE NIGGAS AIN'T LOYAL **I, II & III**

By **Nikki Tee**

THE STREETS BLEED MURDER **I & II**

By **Jerry Jackson**

DIRTY LICKS

By **Peter Mack**

THE ULTIMATE BETRAYAL

By **Phoenix**

BROOKLYN ON LOCK **I & II**

By **Sonovia Alexander**

DON'T FU#K WITH MY HEART **I & II**

By **Linnea**

BOSS'N UP **I & II**

By **Royal Nicole**

LOYALTY IS BLIND

By **Kenneth Chisholm**

I LOVE YOU TO DEATH

By Destiny J

BOOKS BY LDP'S CEO, CA$H

TRUST NO MAN

TRUST NO MAN 2

TRUST NO MAN 3

BONDED BY BLOOD

SHORTY GOT A THUG

A DIRTY SOUTH LOVE

THUGS CRY

THUGS CRY 2

TRUST NO BITCH

TRUST NO BITCH 2

TRUST NO BITCH 3

TIL MY CASKET DROPS

Coming Soon

TRUST NO BITCH (KIAM EYEZ' STORY)

THUGS CRY 3

BONDED BY BLOOD 2

RESTRANING ORDER

NO LOYALTY NO LOVE